Faulty Impressions

Joanne Henning

JD Henning

Cover design: Rebecca Finkel, FPGD.com

A special thanks to the dental school class of 1983, who were the inspiration for this story. This book honors studies, friendships, and struggles during those memorable years in dental school.

Prologue- August 1979

It was incredibly hot in the dental school.

Dean Gallagher rushed from a meeting wearing a suit; he had forgotten about the scheduled air conditioning repair. He removed his jacket and tie before beginning the meeting with John Marlow.

"This matter should be handled with discretion," he insisted in a worried voice. "The dental school has an unblemished reputation under my watch."

"Of course, I understand," replied John Marlow. "The goal is to resolve these problems quickly and quietly."

Marlow is a private investigator and a security specialist hired by the dean; a laid-back Californian who somehow found himself in the Midwest and the owner of a security firm he founded years earlier. A touch of grey at his temples is the only sign of his middle age. Marlow is far more relaxed than the dean; he is cool and competent, with a carefree persona and a casual appearance. Dean Gallagher described events that were most likely a case of theft by an employee or contractor, and Marlow assumed the problems at the dental school were minor compared to some of the shocking cases he had resolved in the past few years.

" Let's tour the dental school," suggested the dean. "I will provide information about daily operations so that you can recommend increased security before the semester begins."

The large, modern-looking structure was four years old with three floors. Marlow and the dean started the tour by descending to the lower level via the staircase. The dean enjoyed showing off the facility.

"This is where the freshman and sophomore students spend most of their time. The labs and classrooms are open after hours for students to finish their lab projects. Campus security locks the building at 10 pm."

Marlow noted the floor had a spacious hallway and an exit at either end. When he looked into the lab rooms, he saw long countertops with chairs for about 80 students. The lower level also housed a cafeteria and four large classrooms. This was a basement level without windows; he imagined it could be closed later than the rest of the building if the underclassmen needed to work late.

The dean eyed the stairs and instead opted for the elevator to return to the second floor, the oppressive heat dictating his decision. "The dental clinic is on the second floor, where the students, juniors, and seniors, treat patients. Each student has a cart with instruments that can move to different assignments or blocks; endodontics, periodontics, crown and bridge..."

"I get the idea," said Marlow. "Is there a problem with theft in the clinic?"

" Surprisingly, no," replied the dean. "We have always been lax in securing the floor since we expect the students to be honest and respectful. I do not think the break-ins involved a student, but I don't know."

Marlow surveyed the clinic floor. Each station has a dental chair, light, and tubing for suction and compressed air. He saw one hundred and fifty units, and a lingering scent reminded him of the dentist's office he went to for treatment.

"We are very proud of the school's state-of-the-art equipment and reputation for excellence," noted the dean. "The students have treated thousands of patients."

They rode up one more level to the third floor. Despite being warm, Marlow felt a chill as soon as the elevator door opened. This level seemed abandoned.

"The third floor is for storage and records. Our business office is here, and research and development share the same space. There is very little traffic on the third floor because the only students who routinely use it are the freshman anatomy students. The lab is to your left; the cadavers are in the room."

Marlow, an ex-cop and private investigator, was not troubled by the cadavers since he often visited the medical examiner when working on cases. Drapes were covering the thirteen souls waiting to be studied by the students.

"Most professors work on the second floor; only Dr. Bloom and Dr. Hall have offices on the third. I don't know why they have been targeted, so you will have to consider all possibilities. I don't care about catching the perpetrators. I just want these disruptions to stop."

Marlow considered the dean's concerns and spent a few minutes developing his approach. "I will need a floor plan of the building and a list of third-floor employees and their activities. I suggest a more secure area for Vicodin, Percocet, and Percodan with constant oversight and detailed records of these medications. Our priority is to secure the building, and if this is done and there are no further incidents, it will be up to you whether you want me to investigate the third-floor staff. So many people come in and out of the building; it may not be possible to figure out what has happened, and the perpetrators may not take further action."

"That sounds like a plan I agree with."

"One more thing, do you trust your cleaning service?"

The dean sighed. "I was unhappy with their performance and failed to renew their contract this year. They were inefficient, and careless, and rarely finished before 4 am."

"Expect the service completion within hours. If you cannot find a cleaning service to finish in a few hours, you will need a security guard overnight."

Dean Gallagher looked defeated. "We do not have the budget for a security guard, and it will be difficult to find a maintenance company with a staff large enough to clean the entire building in a few hours."

"It's time to get creative, Dean Gallagher. I can secure the building, but I need your help to minimize the risk. I will have my estimate and recommendations by next week. Call me when you have the floor plans and employee records, and ask questions in the meantime."

"Thank you for your time, Mr. Marlow."

***

Dean Gallagher hoped operations would run smoothly at the dental school. He had a sinking feeling about the upcoming school year. The vandalism on the third floor was troubling, and the missing pain medications were a grave concern. Dean Gallagher was also receiving complaints about instructors, one in particular, and the complaints had been coming in more frequently. The incoming freshman class was another problem; they were interesting, to say the least, and by far the most diverse class ever enrolled, with two international students, nine women, and out of the 76 enrollees less than half had majored in the sciences. They were the youngest class ever enrolled, and undoubtedly the most immature. Gallagher entered his office and nodded to his secretary, Mrs. Susman.

"Marjorie, could you locate the floor plans for the building? And also get personnel records for employees working in the third-floor offices."

"Right away, Dean Gallagher. Oh, by the way, I just received a certified letter from one of the incoming freshmen. He decided to drop out."

"Already!" roared the dean. "We haven't even started classes yet."

"The student changed his mind and is going to pharmacy school."

"Please bring me the alternate list," he responded with annoyance, "and leave out anyone who applied to one of the other professional schools."

"Yes, sir, right away. I am sure we can find a suitable candidate."

Part I

The Challenge

JD Henning

Chapter 1

Anthony looked like hell, and he felt worse than he looked. The symptoms appeared suddenly; high fever, chills, and nausea. It was just his luck to catch the flu in August. He situated himself on the family room couch so he was close to the bathroom and he could watch TV, and had aspirin, tissues, and a pitcher of water within reach on the coffee table. He sank into the couch, trying to find a comfortable position, when he heard someone fumbling with a key at the front door.

"Go away," he moaned in a weak voice, "you don't want to be near me."

"Tony, are you alright?"

"Yes, Tommy, come in, but don't get too close. I'm certain I am contagious."

"How are you?" Tommy took one look at his younger brother. He looked awful. "Our mother is worried about you. She is pressuring Dad to cut their vacation short; the only thing that stopped her was my promise to look in on you and go shopping for you."

"Thanks, Tommy, I don't want attention. I just want to be left alone."

"I figured as much. She wanted me to pass on instructions: drink plenty of fluids, take lukewarm showers to lower your temperature, and avoid heavy foods."

"Mom doesn't have to worry about the last one. I can't even think about food."

"Well, I won't discuss what I bought at the Hinky Dinky. I will just put it in the fridge, and you can find it when you're ready."

"Thanks, bro."

"I have to hurry to work, but call me if you need anything, and for God's' sake pick up the phone if it rings. If Mom calls to check up on you and you don't answer, she'll be home in a minute."

***

Anthony had two siblings, an older brother, and a younger sister. Tommy was three years older than he was, and a tough act to follow. Tommy was smart, confident, and popular in high school and college; he was the guy who knew everyone; he had a successful job, a beautiful girlfriend, and a luxurious apartment, and people seemed to be drawn to him, especially women. Anthony was not like him; he was shy and liked to stay home and listen to music. They were both athletic, but Tommy was a football star, while Anthony sat on the bench on the high school baseball team. Tommy was a leader, and Anthony was a follower. Anthony felt mediocre when compared to his brother, but the one thing that set Anthony apart was his ambition to become a dentist. His parents encouraged him, and he felt the profession would suit his personality.

His sister Angela adored both of her brothers, but she always joked around with Anthony. He had a fun relationship with his little sister and recognized she was the only female who laughed at his jokes. Her parents were driving her to college, and since she was starting her freshman year, they would help her move in and settle her before they left. Afterward, they planned to vacation at points of interest on the way back. Anthony did not want them to shorten their trip because of his illness. They didn't expect him to be at home when they planned the trip, since they assumed he would be in dental school. Unfortunately, he did not have an offer to attend dental school even though he applied to two schools. The first denied his application, and the second gave him alternate status. This meant that if a student refused an offer, he might get the open spot. He was losing hope; classes would start in two weeks. He resigned himself to finding an alternate job, and his bachelor of science in biology might not help him. To make matters worse, he experienced a disastrous breakup with a girlfriend, and now he was sick with the flu.

Anthony needed an escape from his thoughts and discomfort. He noticed a pink book under the couch and recognized it as the library book he promised Angela he would return for her; he was certain it must be overdue. A romance novel. No surprise there. He hoped Angela was not naïve enough to believe in these fanciful tales, since she was unlikely to find Prince Charming at a fraternity party. Anthony was curious about romance novels, and especially interested in how they depicted the male characters. He expected a hero who was rich, handsome, and an expert swordsman and a passionate lover. His curiosity overcame him, and he picked up the book.

The dynamic between the two main characters amused him, and the mystery intrigued him. The hero was rich and an earl, but far from perfect with a sketchy past, and rumors of indiscretions. His appearance was dark and dangerous, with his intense gaze and a disturbing scar on his chin. In a twist of fate, he met a woman who needed his help. She was 25 and left on the shelf since women were usually married by then in that era. She was not interested in a traditional courtship and therefore was not a suitable marriage prospect for upper-class gentlemen. The earl was taken by her beauty, with her brilliant red hair and luminous green eyes. She didn't consider him dangerous or unapproachable, because he was the most exciting man she had ever met. Despite his questionable reputation, she agreed to embark on a crazy adventure with him, and their experiences eventually brought them together. The steamy passages his little sister must have read embarrassed him, and he thought it best to return the book before his mother saw it.

He spent the rest of the day reading and retired after he finished the book. Could he be dark and dangerous like the guy in the novel? Probably not. As far as women were concerned, Anthony just wasn't that exciting. He was by nature sensitive and reserved, and he imagined most women found him depressingly dull. He was not interested in a casual fling; he wanted a steady girlfriend. In the past, the women he dated lost interest; they thought he was a nice guy but not very exciting, and they didn't want a serious relationship. His mother was the only female who thought he was a 'good catch'. The description disturbed him. He had visions of his second-grade fishing expedition, when he pulled in a sad little sunny with a hook through its lip. He remembered Uncle Mark saying, "Don't worry, Anthony, he doesn't feel the hook," but in his second-grade mind, he thought *Of course he was feeling it* and couldn't wait to release the fish back into the water.

He fell asleep, but the phone ringing the next morning woke him up. He jumped up to answer it, expecting his mother.

"This is Mrs. Susman from the admissions office at the dental school. May I speak to Anthony Roselli?"

Anthony's heart skipped a beat. "Speaking."

"Please hold," said Mrs. Susman." I will connect you to the dean."

"Hello Anthony, this is Dean Gallagher. I am calling you because I have an opening for a first-year student, and I want to offer you the opportunity."

"Yes, I will take it. I appreciate the offer, sir."

The dean smiled to himself. "Well, great. I will be out of town for a few days but would like to meet with you early next week. There are forms to be completed, and we will need your tuition deposit. Can you come in next week?"

"Yes, sir. I am 90 minutes away, I can come in at your convenience."

"I will see you soon. Mrs. Susman will set up a meeting."

"Thank you for the opportunity. If I may ask, is everything alright? I hope the student who dropped out is well."

"The student is fine, he decided to go to pharmacy school instead, so we are glad to have you on board. I will transfer you over to my secretary."

Dean Gallagher had a satisfied feeling. He was sure he had chosen the right applicant.

Chapter 2

The phone call was life-changing, and despite his excitement, the two weeks he had to prepare for his move overwhelmed him. He tried calling Tommy at work to share his news and reached his brother's secretary. She was courteous but screened all phone calls.

"Mr. Roselli is in a meeting, but he should be able to call back around noon. Can I take a message?"

"This is not urgent, but leave him a message from his brother, Anthony. Let him know I just got accepted into dental school."

"Congratulations. I hear it's hard to get in."

"It was for me. I will be home all day; have him call when he has the time."

"Sure thing, and best of luck!"

"Thanks."

Anthony didn't waste time trying to find a place to live. He called student housing and the administrative offices of all four professional schools. Though he hoped to live within walking distance of the school, he would settle for a commute if he ended up a few miles away. He waited for return phone calls, and when the phone rang, he promptly picked up.

"Is Dr. Roselli in?"

"I like the sound of that, Tommy, but it's premature."

Tommy was thrilled. Even though he busted his little brother regularly, he was Anthony's greatest advocate.

"I am looking for a place to live near the dental school. Any suggestions?"

"Let me think." Tommy knew people from school and through his business associations. After a pause, he had an idea. "There is a guy I know from fraternity days. He rents a house near the hospital and the dental school, and when I ran into him six months ago, he was still living there. I'll give him a call and see if he has a room to rent."

"Sounds great, Tommy. Do you think he'd have a problem living with a student? I'm rather desperate; even if he could put me up for a month or two, it would help."

"I don't think Chuck would mind a student, as he still looks and acts like a college guy. He's a jazz enthusiast, and kind of quirky. His name is Chuck Meadow. He was a blast at parties, but I haven't socialized with him for years. Just a warning; he's a little eccentric."

"What do you mean?"

"That's all I have to say. If you meet him, you'll see."

"Okay."

***

Anthony drove to the dental school the following Tuesday. His parents hadn't returned from their trip, but they spoke to him and were ecstatic with the news. As he approached the school, he noted the surrounding residential housing, which looked like older two-story dwellings built on small lots. The homes were small but well cared for, and the streets had well-maintained sidewalks. As he approached his destination, the area became more commercial. He parked near three large modern-looking buildings that were connected by a skywalk, one over the road behind the hospital and the other over a parking lot for the health sciences library. The dental school was in the middle and connected to both buildings. Since Anthony arrived an hour early, he toured the library, which was by far the most interesting building on campus. The three floors had a large open space in the center, separated by rows and rows of books. It looked like a factory, with indoor brick, colored pipes, and large ceiling fans that lined the vaulted ceiling. Many student desks were traditional, but the facility offered study carrels with large tables and lounge areas with beanbag chairs. The interior was open and decorated in bold, bright colors, and Anthony imagined he would spend many hours in the library. He felt fortunate to have access to it.

After arriving at the dental school, he registered; the process was uneventful. Dean Gallagher was a big man with kind eyes and a firm handshake who seemed pleased to meet his new applicant, and Anthony felt like he had an ally in the dean's office. Mrs. Susman was also very nice; professional, pleasant, and very efficient. When he left, he was optimistic about his future.

The next step was to find Chuck's house at 439 Wisteria Lane. The house was four blocks from the dental school and was on a small lot, a narrow colonial with a front porch. There was a sign in the window. What did it say? 'Michelob'. It was a sign that would light up at night. He rechecked the house number. He heard loud music. Jazz. He knocked on the door. Then he knocked louder. As the door opened, a shrill barking and a large black dog greeted him.

"Down, Ralphie!" implored his owner. The dog was wagging its tail and grinning, with its large tongue lolling out of its mouth. Anthony knew the dog would pounce as soon as the door opened. "I said sit Ralphie!" The dog ignored its owner and jumped up immediately to welcome their guest.

"I'm sorry. He's friendly but has no manners. Hi, I'm Chuck. You must be Tony."

They tried to shake hands as Ralphie was jumping about. The pup was so excited he was peeing on the floor. Anthony, who liked dogs, grabbed his collar and guided him into a sitting position. "Sit." The startled canine was so surprised he obeyed.

" How did you do that?"

"You have to show him you are the alpha dog, let him know you're the boss. He seems eager to please; I'm sure it wouldn't be hard to train him. How old is he?"

"He's about 7 months old, a puppy mentally but nearly full grown."

"I'm sure with some training he will follow your orders." Anthony did not know a canine resident was part of the equation, but he liked dogs and tried to view the opportunity with an open mind. They walked into a large living room, and Anthony noticed four couches that did not match.

"Is this a frat house, Chuck?"

"Oh, no. I graduated in the same class as your brother 3 years ago. The couches come in handy when I have guests."

Anthony thought that was a weird comment but didn't ask. A small bathroom was located downstairs next to a kitchen with a full-sized refrigerator, oven, and stove, and a large table. The room was bright and sunny, with red countertops and hardwood floors. It looked clean and rarely used. In the corner sat Ralphie's water dish and bed.

Chuck led the way toward the staircase. "Come upstairs; I'll show you the room for rent."

As they ascended a narrow staircase, Anthony noticed a dizzying pattern on the wall. The black design was fuzzy as Anthony touched the wall.

"Did you decorate the place, Chuck?"

"No, it was like this when I started renting 3 years ago. I don't know how I ended up with so many couches; people just kept dropping them off."

Anthony once again ignored the odd remark. Chuck showed him a side room to the right of the stairs. It was small, with a window that looked over the street. The hardwood floor was the best feature, and someone furnished the room with a dresser and small desk.

"Is there a bed?"

"No, but if we can get it up the steps, you can use one couch." Anthony sighed. He was desperate. The location was perfect. Though disorganized, Chuck seemed to keep the place clean.

"So here's the deal," said Chuck. "The rent is $110 per month and half the utilities. It is mostly quiet in the house, but I have musician friends who come over to jam. I need a roommate who doesn't mind Ralphie and will occasionally pitch in with his care. You can have the room for the school year, or long enough to find another place."

Anthony hesitated. He was concerned about the noise potential of this residence. "What instrument do you play, Chuck?"

"Saxophone. How about you?"

"I love music, but I'm afraid I have no talent."

" Come now, there must be something you're good at."

"No, really, there isn't." An awkward silence hung in the air. He tried to be honest with Chuck. "I'm chill, but require solid sleep on weekdays."

A pause. Chuck liked Anthony and tried to be more accommodating. "Did I mention I just opened a jazz club on the main road? Right now it's open from Thursday to Sunday night so you can have the house to yourself on those nights, except for Ralphie of course."

That was a plus for Anthony since he was interested in solitude so he could study. He was ready to seal the deal but had one more question.

"I saw a bathroom but no shower. Is there a bathroom upstairs?"

"Of course, let me show you the rest of the house."

Anthony peeked into Chuck's room, which was a little larger than the spare bedroom. The walls displayed posters of Santana and Chick Corea in concert. Then Anthony walked into the main bathroom. The wallpaper was lime green and lemon yellow striped, and the fixtures were avocado green. There was a shower, a tub, and a psychedelic design on the shower curtain. The door had striped wallpaper like the walls, so when it was shut it looked like there was no door.

"Have you ever gotten lost in this bathroom, Chuck?"

He replied with a chuckle. "Don't go in when you're drunk; you might not find your way out."

Anthony smiled. "The place has character. I'll take the room. Thanks, Chuck."

Chapter 3

The taxi passed the dental school and turned left. After traveling 5 blocks, it stopped at a large two-story colonial house with an outdoor staircase to the second floor. Rebecca Monahan thanked the taxi driver as she hauled her large suitcase onto the sidewalk. She arrived several days early and was thankful to have the dreaded trip behind her. She hated flying. Her next-door neighbors and close friends, Ellen and Donna, did not expect her until the end of the week, so she wanted to surprise them with her arrival. She noticed a flurry of activity around the outdoor staircase. Bees. She stared at the swarming insects with disbelief; she had only been gone a few weeks, and they had set up shop and made a home for themselves while she was away.

She rang the doorbell of the downstairs tenants. The Grillis were always home, and she heard Mr. Grilli playing a Frank Sinatra album. She rang the doorbell again and Mrs. Grilli finally answered the door.

"Rebecca, welcome back!"

Mrs. Grilli was in a housecoat, but as usual, her hair and makeup were perfect, and she wore expensive jewelry. Mrs. Grilli put in so much effort for a woman who didn't drive and rarely left her house.

"I hate to bother you, but do you have any bee spray? I can't get into my apartment, they are swarming around the steps."

"I will go ask my husband." After a few minutes, Mrs. Grilli returned with a spray can. "Vinnie says you should wait until it's dark to use this. Wear long sleeves and long pants and spray when they are sleeping."

"Tell Mr. Grilli thanks for the spray and the advice."

Rebecca didn't expect Mrs. Grilli to ask her in. Mr. Grilli was a bit of a recluse. Rebecca, living upstairs for a year, heard him but never saw him. She was well-versed in his taste for music, as he always had an album on. Rebecca didn't mind his choices, but everything he played was at least 20 years old. The couple did not drive and did not go outside, and she often wondered how they got their groceries.

Rebecca dragged her suitcase towards the house next door. Her friend Ellen spotted her and raced down her steps to greet her.

"Rebecca, you're back! Why didn't you call me? I could have picked you up from the airport." Ellen gave Rebecca a big hug and a questioning look as she picked up the suitcase. "Are you locked out of your apartment?"

"It's a long story," sighed Rebecca.

"Could you come upstairs and tell me about it? I'm cleaning my closet and realize I should buy a few new items for school. Would you be up for a trip to the mall?"

"Sure, since I am here early, I have plenty of time to go shopping."

Ellen looked at Rebecca. "Your hair looks gorgeous; it makes you look so sophisticated."

"Thanks, Ellen. It was my first step toward looking more professional. I thought the long hair tied back in a ponytail made me look too young."

Rebecca had silky red hair that was straight and almost to her waist. She had worn it in a simple style, parted on the side, and tied it back when she treated patients in the dental clinic. Over break, in a bold move, she had it cut shoulder length and added subtle blond highlights. The face frame brought attention to her delicate features.

"You'll have to beat off those lonely guys in the dental school," teased Ellen.

"I'm not worried about that. The guys in my class have steered clear of involvement with the women in the class. If there were ever any interest, they would surely keep it to themselves. I doubt they would notice a change."

"Well, I'm sure someone will notice the change; I certainly did, but are you looking, Rebecca? What about Kyle?"

Kyle was Rebecca's boyfriend in New Jersey. She had met him during a summer when she was at home and had dated him for two years. She had become so distraught with the relationship she decided to cut her summer vacation short and return to school early. "He's changed. He quit graduate school to focus full time on his band and thinks he's destined for fame and fortune, but the band has only booked small local gigs."

"Did you guys break up?"

"No, Ellen, but maybe we should have. This relationship has been strained, and long distance has not worked for us. The glamour of being the bass player's girlfriend has certainly worn off for me. I'm also sure he has been dating other women while I'm here at school."

"Oh, Rebecca, I'm sorry."

Rebecca had resigned herself to reality. "Even though there was no formal breakup, I think it's over for us. It doesn't feel the same."

"Is that why you came back early?"

"Yes, to get away from Kyle and all his problems. And I could not get into my apartment because the entrance is infested. Mr. Grilli said

I should wait until nightfall to spray the yellow jackets since they are inactive at night."

"You talked to Mr. Grilli?"

"No, I got the bee spray through Mrs. Grilli. I still haven't seen him."

"Have dinner here tonight, and we'll conquer those varmints later. Donna won't be back until tomorrow. Why don't you spend the night and move into your apartment in the morning?"

Donna and Ellen were Rebecca's next-door neighbors. The three women had been friends in undergraduate and now attended professional school; Donna in law school, Ellen in medical school, and Rebecca in dental school. They studied in different circles but remained close friends and neighbors. Rebecca stayed at Ellen's apartment that night and entered her own apartment in the morning.

Chapter 4

The end of August was a whirlwind for Anthony. He moved in with Chuck, and they carried one couch to the second floor. Anthony, tall at six foot three, could stretch out on the longest couch. The Friday before classes was an orientation for the freshman dental students. The freshmen had assigned seats in the lab; seated alphabetically. He recognized a few guys from undergraduate classes, but Amy White was the only student he knew well; she was from his hometown in Iowa, and he had known her since second grade.

He looked around the room at the other freshmen and noticed the clean-cut, professional students in the front of the room. Most candidates looked like they could be dentists, but as the alphabet progressed his classmates looked more diverse, relaxed, and unconventional. Six students were in Anthony's anatomy group, and they were a motley crew. Anthony sat next to Joe Reilly, a guy he knew from undergraduate; a tall, friendly Irishman who looked like a lumberjack with red hair and a beard. He had huge hands. Anthony wondered how that would work out with a future in dentistry. Pinkish Singh was the other guy sitting next to him. He was from India, and though he could speak English well, he often sounded awkward because the words seemed out of sequence and he was sometimes unfamiliar with the subtleties of American slang. Anthony expected to have some interesting conversations with him. Roy Tanoa was next in line, a casual laid-back guy from Hawaii who wore flip-flops, and at the end of the alphabet was Ron Zee, with his long hair and tinted glasses he looked like he belonged in a rock band rather than in this dental school group. Amy White sat between Roy and Ron. She was attractive and knew it— a petite blond with big blue eyes; she was a head turner, a heartbreaker, a former prom queen, and a cheerleader. Anthony knew her well and was grateful Roy and Pinkish provided a buffer between them.

Anyone who expected a cheerful welcome at orientation was mistaken. The curriculum seemed impossible, and Anthony suspected the instructors disliked the back row. After several announcements, they toured the dental school with their anatomy group. Mrs. Susman was there to give the freshmen instructions. "Arrive on Monday at 8 am and follow the schedule provided today. There is a 45-minute lunch break. The cafeteria has a soft drink machine, a coffee machine, and a full-sized refrigerator. You can bring lunch or go to the cafeteria on the main campus. If you use the refrigerator, make sure your items have your name on them. The students who signed up for work-study in the dental school should return to this room for a meeting at 10:30. Jeff Muller, a third-year student, is in charge and will discuss your work assignment. Enjoy the tour of the school. The dean's office is open if you have questions, and we look forward to the start of your semester on Monday."

After dismissal, Anthony, Joe, Pinkish, Amy, Roy, and Ron walked around the dental school. They anticipated two years of study and lab work. After learning skills on the lower level of the building, they would move to the second-floor clinic to treat patients. The tour was pleasant until they reached the third floor. The students were silent as they entered the anatomy lab and were 'introduced' to the person they would dissect. There was a sheet over the cadaver, but his arm was visible since the first assignment would be dissection of the arm. Anthony glanced over at Amy to see how she was handling it. Of course, she was fine, tougher than most of the male students. She was a biology major, too. The mood was strangely quiet in the lab, but the conversation exploded when they reached the hallway.

"I guess we'll get used to it," said Joe Reilly.

"Of course we will," added Roy. "We should be able to do this since we will someday have to drill people's teeth."

"I am not experienced in dissection," warned Pinkish; " I fear my contribution will be almost zero."

"Who majored in biology?" asked Ron.

Amy and Anthony admitted they were biology majors.

"When it's a person, it's different," Anthony cautioned. "The only mammal Amy and I have dissected was a cat."

Amy had a cavalier attitude. "Come on, guys, it's part of the program. How difficult could it be?"

Anthony distanced himself from the group and was several steps behind them, lost in his thoughts. He didn't want to make a big deal about being a biology major. They were all better students than he was; after all, he was sure he was the last candidate to be accepted. He turned to look at the third-floor offices. That is when he saw her. A vision. She was the most intriguing woman he had ever laid eyes on. She looked like a siren with her red hair ... no, wait, more like an angel with her dainty features and the golden highlights that framed her face. He suspected she was both. His heart skipped a beat, and he had to catch his breath. He feasted his eyes for a moment, then turned and continued with his group. He could only dream of a woman like that. She was definitely out of his league.

He was so enthralled by the girl on the third floor that he almost forgot about the work-study meeting. Pinkish reminded him by asking if he planned to head back to the freshman lab. Twelve students attended the meeting. Jeff Mueller described the job that involved maintenance at the dental school from 5 pm to 7 pm, Monday through Friday. Jeff had organized a schedule for his crew.

"I will assign you to a floor: five will be working on the first floor, five on the second, and two on the third, which has light traffic and requires less upkeep."

Jeff read the assignments and got to the last two names on the list. "Roselli, Singh, third floor."

Pinkish looked at Anthony. "We are in alliance?"

"Yes, it looks like we are a team. How are your cleaning skills?"

"Excellent!"

He was happy to be paired with Pinkish. They were both hard workers and energetic. Anthony thought he might help Pinkish Americanize his verbal skills and hoped he could meet the attractive redhead working on the third floor.

Chapter 5

Rebecca Monahan was the senior student hired to be Dr. Bloom's teaching assistant for the dental materials class for sophomores. Dr. Bloom needed a proficient writer and editor for a dental materials newsletter and a student to coordinate his lecture notes. The dental field was changing because of acid etching and enamel bonding. Because the recommendations were fluid, his lecture material needed an update, and he asked Rebecca to compose timely notes on the latest innovations.

Rebecca relished the opportunity to be a TA and recognized it as a chance to cultivate her writing talents and apply them to dentistry. She knew her assignment would be time-consuming, but the extra work would not interfere with her clinical requirements. The only downside was that she would share an office with Dr. Hall, her freshman anatomy professor. She disliked him and tried to stay clear of him. Dr. Hall acted as a roadblock to the success of the freshman anatomy students, and some of those struggling dropped out of dental school because of his courses. Although Rebecca passed his classes freshman year, her study partner did not, and he was no longer in school because of failing grades in Dr. Hall's courses. Whenever she thought about her friend, she had an ache in her heart; he would have been a fine dentist.

Rebecca and two other women worked on the third floor: Judy, the hygiene instructor, and Dr. Hall's new assistant, Mia Reynolds. Judy and Rebecca avoided Dr. Hall and wondered how the new assistant would tolerate his moods and demands. Rebecca did not work during business hours, so she would not see Judy or Mia other than in passing.

Judy was happy to see Rebecca working on the third floor before the start of the semester. "How was your summer, Rebecca? Are you relieved to be a senior?"

"The summer was enjoyable, and yes, I am glad the year will be mostly in the clinic treating patients. I am the teaching assistant for Dr. Bloom this year and will be in this office working for him."

"Well, welcome to the third floor."

Just then, Dr. Hall walked in. "Hello Ms. Monahan, this is a surprise. Have you come to visit me?"

Rebecca glanced at Judy, who was behind him. Judy rolled her eyes and made a face; Rebecca tried to ignore this and looked straight at Dr. Hall. "I'm here for Dr. Bloom."

"Perhaps you could do some work for me."

"Don't you have a full-time assistant, Dr. Hall?"

" Yes, but I like to surround myself with helpful ladies."

"I am sure you will not see much of me, Dr. Hall. I cannot arrive until I finish at the clinic, and you will probably leave before five. I assume your wife will expect you for dinner."

Dr. Hall raised his eyebrows in a disparaging glare. She didn't care; she had to make it clear she was not interested in him and that he should leave her alone. Rebecca had other reasons to be squeamish about the third floor. She didn't like to think about the year she spent dissecting cadavers and the floor housed thirteen dead people. They were across the hallway, and she would hate to be alone with them. Rebecca imagined there would be janitors, but she might feel uneasy since she didn't know them. Undaunted, she set aside these concerns, made notes and suggestions for Dr. Bloom, and left for the day.

***

On her way home, Rebecca visited Anna, a tall blond girl from California, who was her best friend in the clinic. Their friendship grew as they faced the challenging and sometimes awkward interactions with their instructors. Anna lived very close to school, and the house she rented with other dental students was a convenient detour for Rebecca. She couldn't wait to see her friend Anna after summer break and discuss her upsetting encounter with Dr. Hall.

"Rebecca, I missed you!" Anna exclaimed as she hugged her friend.

"One more year to go; I can't imagine it being worse than the first three."

"Oh, we're just used to it now, Anna."

"I love your hair, Rebecca. Maybe you should quit school and become a model."

"At 25, I'm sure I'm too old for modeling. Do you like it?"

"Very much. But we don't seem to get noticed, regardless of what we do."

"You can say that again!"

"We should enjoy our freedom this weekend while we can. Do you want to go out tonight?"

"Sure, I want to tell you about my weird conversation with Dr. Hall. Just think, Monday is the beginning of the end."

"That's something to celebrate. I'll pick you up at ten, Rebecca."

***

The girls decided on a local brewery that served beer, drinks, and peanuts. The floor was littered with peanut shells. They did not see familiar faces, so they sat at the bar and talked about summer break. Rebecca spoke about her troubles with Kyle and her reservations about working on the third- floor office with Dr. Hall. As soon as Anna suggested Rebecca should start dating again, a professional-looking guy in his thirties approached them. He conversed with both women for several minutes and was pleasant, talkative, and good-looking. When he asked Rebecca out, she took Anna's advice and agreed to dinner plans for the following Friday night.

That weekend, the students tried to prepare for a Monday start. Some partied, getting in the last bit of summer break before being swamped with their studies. Others rested, trying to prepare for the lack of sleep that would plague them once they started the academic year. Chuck invited Anthony to the jazz club, but he declined and promised to go the following weekend. He wanted to visit the club, but needed time to settle in. Anthony planned to use his room as an office. He removed the sheets, blanket, and pillows from the closet to make his bed at night, and in the morning he put the bedding back into the closet.

He was nervous about starting school, so to keep his mind occupied he spent part of the weekend training Ralphie. Ralphie learned how to sit and shake hands. He learned to stay when his meal was served. This routine helped, but the pup still inhaled his food when given permission. Anthony didn't think he could slow him down. Chuck was pleased. His pet was finally learning some manners.

8 am Monday came all too soon.

Chapter 6

High stacks of textbooks covered their lab stations, with each book containing over 600 pages. The titles were 'Pathology', 'Microbiology', 'Biochemistry', 'Anatomy',' Dental Anatomy', 'Head and Neck Anatomy', 'Embryology', 'The Human Nervous System', and 'Emergencies in the Dental Office,' which was the only paperback. The amount of material was staggering. Anthony would need a shopping cart to carry these books to Chuck's house at the end of the day. Dissections started, and his anatomy group selected Anthony to begin the project. The human arm is complex. The circulatory and nervous systems have many components, and they had many muscles to identify. Careful dissection was crucial because if someone mistakenly cut a structure, they would find it difficult to use its pathway for identification. Anthony felt they would not have enough time to study this arm since the lab practical was in October.

Every time Anthony went up to the third floor, he looked into the office of Dr. Hall and Dr. Bloom. He sometimes saw two women packing up to leave work, but not the gorgeous redhead he saw during orientation. His anatomy professor noticed his curiosity, annoyed by the intrusion. Anthony was already wary of Dr. Hall, who had a notorious reputation amongst the students; he seemed to enjoy mocking them and treated their questions with disdain. Anthony had the impression Dr. Hall was full of himself; a pompous ass. Amy was the only one in their group willing to ask him questions, and Anthony hoped she had the common sense to keep her distance.

Anthony was becoming overwhelmed with the information, and the subjects started to blur together. There were not enough hours in the day to attend classes and do the suggested reading. In addition to his studies, he had dental anatomy lab projects to complete and spent many hours studying the anatomy of specific teeth. They started with the maxillary right central incisor, front view, back view, side view, incisal view. He drew the central incisor from different angles, carved the central incisor out of soap, and carved the central incisor out of plaster. Anthony started to dream about the central incisor. His anxiety was apparent to him when he had a recurring nightmare. He dreamt he was eating an apple and his central incisor fell out of his mouth and into the apple. Dr. Hall was there, laughing. He then woke up in a sweat.

***

At the end of a busy Thursday, Dr. Bloom asked Rebecca to type the updated lecture for the following week and print copies. She had to stay at the clinic late that day. When she entered the third-floor office, she was alone, and it was quiet. She occasionally heard the janitor's cart moving about. But then she heard music, and the dismal third floor seemed to have a party atmosphere. The guys working had a boombox, and excellent taste in music. She heard a jazzy, soulful voice that seemed closer to her than the recording. A familiar song; *'Ain't No Sunshine,'* sung with such depth, such feeling, she was certain the vocalist was digging deep into his own emotions. This voice was marvelous, yet haunting. She was tempted to put her arms around this man. Who was he? She spent many hours listening to Kyle on stage, and not once did he project such passion, such a sense of longing and loneliness. Was it the janitor? She peered out of the office, but he had disappeared when she reached the hallway. She finished her notes for the day and left, haunted by the voice.

***

Rebecca's date was on Friday night. He planned dinner at an exclusive restaurant, so she dressed up. Rebecca wore a black dress with black pumps and accessorized with a gold chain necklace and hoop earrings. When she looked in the mirror, she knew Anna was right. She could have been a model. But the truth was that Rebecca had been a late bloomer and never thought she was attractive enough to model. She suffered growing pains in high school and didn't have enough confidence to date until she was in her twenties.

Her date planned an impressive evening. He arrived on time, brought her flowers, and drove her to an elegant restaurant with a marvelous view of the city. Her date was well-spoken and easy to talk to, but she couldn't ignore the uncomfortable feeling in her gut. Something about him didn't seem right. He was too eager to give her his business card, and he told her to call him at his office. Rebecca would never ask for his number unless they dated seriously; she was old-fashioned and always waited for the man to call her. But if he gave out his number, why not his home? She tried to ignore her reservations; she told herself she was nervous about being on a first date. The dinner was wonderful, and they started with a dinner drink, followed by filet mignon with a salad and baked potato. For dessert, they ordered Irish cream in the coffee. Rebecca intended to go home after dessert since it was past 11 o'clock.

"I enjoyed dinner," she said. "Thank you."

He was not ready to end the evening, so he had a suggestion. "There's a new jazz club in town I discovered recently. Are you interested?"

"That sounds like fun. I like jazz."

When they approached the club, the streets looked familiar. She was certain they were close to the dental school. They sat at the bar since the tables were full. "What's your favorite drink?" he asked.

Did she dare? Why not? "Black Russian." She needed a stiff drink to loosen up since she still felt nervous. They were about to finish their drinks when he stood up.

"Excuse me, Rebecca."

He was gone a long time as she waited for him at the bar. A few more minutes went by. She smiled at the bartender; a friendly guy who knew most of the patrons. He was funny and interesting, with a brilliant smile, something she always noticed. His name was Chuck, and she started talking to him because she thought her date had left. As she sat at the bar, a few guys approached her and offered to buy her a drink, but she told them she was waiting for someone. Rebecca enjoyed the live music. The musicians were talented and masters of improvisation, and Chuck told her they were local guys who came to the club to jam. Chuck performed on the saxophone that night. Even though she enjoyed the music, she felt anxious.

Rebecca ordered another drink, certain she was alone. She used the pay phone to see if Anna or Ellen could pick her up, but no one answered. Conspicuous and a little drunk, she realized she should head home. She wasn't far from her apartment. Chuck saw her concerned look and went over to her.

"Are you okay?" he asked sympathetically.

"Well, my date seems to have abandoned me, but the Black Russians have made the situation easier to take."

" I rarely talk about my patrons, but I have seen that guy before. I think he came here with his wife."

"He's married?" Rebecca gasped, shocked. He didn't wear a ring.

"You didn't know?"

"Of course not. I never go out with married men. Is his wife here? Is that what happened?"

"I see the brother-in-law sitting over there."

They both looked at the nearby table of men.

"Would you like me to call you a cab?"

"No, I think I am only a few blocks from my apartment. I'll walk."

"I can't let you do that," warned Chuck. "It's not safe for you to walk in this neighborhood at night, and I am responsible for you because I served you those Black Russians."

Just then, Anthony strolled in and waved to Chuck. He stopped short when he saw Rebecca and gazed at her with unmistakable admiration. Then, Chuck had a brilliant idea and introduced them.

"This is my roommate, Anthony. I'm sorry, I don't know your name."

"Rebecca."

Chuck looked at Anthony and winked. "Rebecca, Anthony is very trustworthy, like a Boy Scout. You would be safer with him than any other guy in this establishment, myself included. I expect he would escort you home if you are comfortable doing that."

Rebecca smiled at Chuck's roommate. She hesitated. "I think that would be fine."

Anthony was stunned. He escorted Rebecca out of the jazz club. "My car is a few blocks away. I walked here."

Once again, she hesitated. She didn't want to get in a car with a guy she didn't know on the recommendation of a bartender she didn't know.

"Do you mind if we walk? My apartment is only a few blocks from here."

"What's the address?"

"694 Degelman Drive."

"I know the street; it's two blocks over."

"And the apartment," added Rebecca, "is five blocks from the dental school."

"No problem," said Anthony. "I have seen you at the dental school."

"Really?" Rebecca was confused. Anthony seemed somehow familiar, but she didn't recognize him. They walked in silence. A cool breeze was rustling through the tree-lined lane. The moon was full.

"The moon looks beautiful tonight," she commented.

"Quite beautiful." He was not looking at the moon but at her, enchanted by the moonlight dancing off the highlights in her hair.

"I miss the fall weather back east."

"I recognize the accent," he said. "New Jersey?"

"How did you know?"

"My family is from New Jersey," replied Anthony. "My parents moved when I was in first grade. The New Jersey shore is the best. The happiest memories were with my cousins at the beach." He paused and looked at her. "So you're a Jersey girl."

Rebecca took a good look at Anthony for the first time. He was quite handsome. He was tall with tousled dark hair, and blue eyes that were warm and inviting when she looked past his glasses. She noticed a tiny scar on his chin. When he smiled, she took notice. His teeth weren't just straight; they were exquisitely shaped. His smile was fabulous. He was smiling at her now.

"So what do you like about Jersey and the beach?" she asked.

"Most people see crashing waves and stay out of the water. But the people from New Jersey dive right in headfirst. They learn at an early age how to handle the waves. It's been years since I've been there, but I miss the waves, the beach, the boardwalk."

"So do I. I don't get back as often as I'd like. When I was a kid, I used to stay in the water all day, and my parents would have to drag me out."

Anthony wanted to ask Rebecca more about herself, but she suddenly turned to him and took his hands. She took a deep breath and looked upset.

"This is so embarrassing, Anthony, but my date left me at the jazz club."

"You're kidding. Was he crazy?" Then he noted her distressed look and took a more serious tone. "The guy must have been a jerk."

Then his voice became so gentle it took her by surprise. "I never would have left you for a minute, Rebecca."

There was something shockingly intimate about this remark and the soft way he said it. His voice was captivating. He was incredibly sexy. She smiled and tried to compose herself. She stumbled over a curb, and he caught her, then walked to her apartment with his arm around her. A long outdoor staircase led to the apartment door, and he walked her to the steps.

"Here we are. Do you need my help with anything else?"

"I'm fine."

She started up the stairs, and Anthony heard her keys tumble off the landing to the ground. He called up to her.

"Don't worry, I'll find them."

Her intoxication kept her from opening her apartment door. He was able to find the right key and open the door for her, but could not take his gaze off of her. Rebecca's eyes were the color of the Caribbean, and her smile lit up the moonlit night. But he had to keep his innermost desires in check. His mission tonight was to make sure she was safe, even from him, and she drank too much to make any rational decisions about inviting him in.

"Thank you, Anthony."

And then she put her hands around his neck and pulled him toward her. Her kiss was passionate, stunning him; then, he couldn't help but kiss her back. He gave himself up to the kiss. She was intoxicating.

She turned and stumbled into her apartment. He stood in the doorway and thought he heard water running in the bathroom.

"Are you feeling well enough, ... I mean, do you think you can manage?" he asked.

"Yes, Anthony, thank you for walking me home."

"I am going to lock the door. Latch it after I leave."

"I'll do that."

He realized she might not remember him. Still, he felt obligated to call in the morning. He scanned the area for her phone, expecting to find her phone number printed on the dial. Rebecca was unorganized, but on her cluttered kitchen counter he found a phone, a pen, and paper- then couldn't help but notice a letter. He knew he shouldn't read it. The small, bold printing looked like male penmanship.

'In anticipation; I want you so much, Love, Kyle.'

Anthony wished he had not seen the letter. So what did he know about Rebecca? Her date abandoned her at the jazz club. A letter from Kyle, who wanted her. Although she didn't know Anthony, she had already kissed him with such uninhibited passion that he was certain he would lay awake thinking about it. She was a red-haired siren who could be more trouble than any woman he had ever known, and his inexperienced heart knew he would be better off forgetting the entire incident. But he somehow couldn't help himself. He was interested.

Chapter 7

The next morning, Rebecca stumbled into the bathroom and looked in the mirror. She was hungover, so wasted last night she didn't even brush her teeth.As she was brushing and flossing, she heard the phone ring, and rinsed out and rushed to answer it. She missed the call anyway. Could it be that cheating married jerk she went to dinner with? Surely, he wouldn't have the balls to contact her after last night's fiasco.

Anthony let the phone ring five times, then hung up. Maybe she was sleeping. She might have a terrible headache. Chuck was in the kitchen, as Ralphie danced about in excitement.

"Hey, Tony. Why didn't you come back to the club last night? Too much fun with the hot redhead?"

" I'm a Boy Scout, remember? I walked her home and then walked here to hang out with Ralphie."

"Is she a neighbor? Go over to borrow a cup of sugar."

"Funny Chuck. She was messed up last night, but I would like to get acquainted under better circumstances."

"You know, Tony, despite what you saw last night, I think she's a nice girl. She was on a date when the guy's brother-in-law walked in. The dirtbag escaped out the back before he was seen. She didn't know he was married. What a slimeball; he just left her there. At least five guys approached her at the bar, and she politely let them know she was with someone. She waited for him until I told her I thought the guy was married and had left the club. She tried calling her friends for a ride but couldn't reach them."

"She was upset on the walk home, but she was nice. She's a Jersey girl, and I think she works at the dental school, but I didn't get to ask."

"Tongue-tied, Tony?"

"Something like that. The situation was unexpected."

***

Rebecca was having tea when she heard a knock at the door. Ellen was peeking through the curtains.

"Hi, Rebecca. You look green this morning."

"Remind me not to go out on any more dates."

"That good, huh?"

"Ellen, it was awful. It started out promising, but then we went to that new jazz club and he left me there."

"That's ridiculous! Did you argue?"

"No, the weasel sneaked out because he saw his brother-in-law."

Ellen gasped. "He's married?"

"Yes, surprise, surprise. A cheater doesn't wear the ring. I've had it with men, older men anyway. Too many of them are married or emotionally unavailable."

"It seems like we've had more than our share of heartache, Rebecca. It's a good thing you found out on the first date."

Rebecca sighed and looked at Ellen. Poor Ellen was dealing with a broken engagement. Being in medical school could ruin relationships.

"How did you get home last night?"

"That's the crazy part of the story. Chuck the bartender told me he suspected my date was a married man who cut out the back door. I didn't want to take a cab, so Chuck's roommate walked me to my apartment. He said he recognized me from the dental school and seemed familiar, but I don't know why."

"Didn't you ask him?"

"I was drunk. I was concentrating on not falling and making a fool of myself."

" Was he interesting? Did you get his name, address, phone number?"

"Only a first name and no. I'll probably never see him again."

"If he saw you at the dental school, he could be a patient. You must be the only female dentist with red hair."

"I know I'm the only one. He sounded familiar..."

"What did he look like?"

Rebecca sighed. "Tall, dark, and handsome, boyish face, blue eyes, dimples, an intoxicating smile; interesting."

"Well, it sounds like the evening wasn't a complete waste. You should have gotten his number." Ellen looked at Rebecca and wondered if she should lie down. "Are you well enough to shop for groceries? Mrs. Capalini is going to the Hinky Dinky with me, and I wondered if you would like to come with us."

"Sure, give me a few minutes. I'll feel better if I take an aspirin and get dressed."

Chapter 8

Mrs. Capalini was their landlady, a widow who owned two houses. She immigrated from Italy but struggled with English even though she had lived in the United States for many years. Ellen and Donna lived in the two-bedroom apartment above her, and Rebecca and the Grillis lived in the house next door. Because Mrs. Capalini didn't drive, the girls often helped her with errands. She had a grown son who lived in town, but he was married and busy with work, so it was easier for Mrs. Capalini to rely on the girls for help. They drove in Ellen's Skylark, which had an enormous trunk and plenty of room for groceries. Food shopping with Mrs. Capalini was an adventure. When they arrived at the Hinky Dinky, Mrs. Capalini sprinted towards the shopping carts.

"Here we go!" Ellen smiled.

They all took carts and went their separate ways. Afterwards, Mrs. Capalini approached Rebecca, quite distressed. " My cart ... is stolen!"

Rebecca took Mrs. Capalini by the hand. "I'm sure it's a mistake, Mrs. Capalini. Someone probably took your cart, realized it did not belong to them, and left it."

They passed Ellen, who gave Rebecca a knowing look. Ellen pointed to the frozen food section.

Rebecca took her landlady by the hand. "Let's look in the refrigerated aisle."

"That's it!" she exclaimed. "Check to see if anything is missing."

Rebecca didn't know if something was missing, but she checked. "There's milk, eggs, and vegetables. I see you have oatmeal and fruit. Is there anything else you need?"

"No. I have everything else at home."

Rebecca and Mrs. Capalini walked to the front of the Hinky Dinky. Their landlady watched as the clerk weighed the vegetables. She was determined to get the right price. "Try that again, miss. I think you overcharge by two cents." Once she had purchased her groceries, she had little patience for waiting around. Ellen and Rebecca grabbed their essentials and purchased their groceries. Their landlady was on the move. When they put their bags in the trunk, Mrs. Capalni took them by the hand. "Nice girls," she said with a smile.

***

Rebecca was exhausted when she returned with her groceries, but pleased the task was done. She gratefully settled into her cozy kitchen but looked around at the clutter that had already accumulated in less than two weeks. When clean, the apartment was just the way she wanted it to be. She missed the four seasons back east, and since the midwestern spring and fall were very short, she decorated her apartment with the four seasons in mind to alleviate her homesickness. She had four rooms, one for each season. The kitchen was like summer: bright, sunny, and spacious, with a large kitchen table that came with the apartment. The walls were pale yellow, the linoleum white, and pale blue countertops sat under pristine white cabinets.

She accessorized with dishtowels that had lemons embroidered on the borders. As you walked out of the kitchen, the living room had cream-colored walls and an earthy brown shag rug. Rebecca had purchased a comfortable brown couch and a TV on a movable stand. She added autumn colors; orange, red, and yellow accents decorated the room. To the right of the living room was a bathroom with a large freestanding claw-foot tub that was white porcelain with a mint green exterior. Rebecca painted the bathroom; she chose a pale winter blue, accessorized with ice blue towels with happy penguins embroidered in the center. On Friday nights, she would move the TV stand so she could watch during a long soak in the tub. She usually watched two shows on Friday nights, *Remington Steele* and D*allas.* The last room in the apartment was her bedroom. It was spacious, with a large window overlooking the street. The hardwood floors and white Battenburg curtains would match anything, so she chose a pastel spring flower print for the bed. The four seasons were in her apartment, and the atmosphere made her happy and comforted her during the long, brutal winters that were a way of life in this area.

On a day like this, she enjoyed her solitude. She brewed a fresh pot of coffee and decided to clean and organize the kitchen before going to bed early. The first thing to go would be Kyle's letters. She gave them a final look. His flowery prose now seemed so insincere, and in hindsight, she realized Kyle was full of theatrics. She could honestly say it had never been love.

She fantasized about her dream man. Her tastes had changed. She thought she might prefer a guy who didn't speak English, maybe someone who could cook and warm her bed at night. No arguing, no hurt feelings, no silly games, no bullshit. Kyle's letters were tossed into the trash. She would have preferred a bonfire, but the garbage can would have to do. She sprinkled coffee grounds on top of the letters so she wouldn't look again, since she was determined and wouldn't have a change of heart. It was time to move on.

Chapter 9

As the weeks flew by, dental school became a monotonous routine. Dental school was a marathon, and pacing yourself was important. Anthony attended classes from 8 am to 5 pm, worked as a custodian from 5 pm to 7 pm, and from 7 pm to midnight he read and studied, then after 7 hours of sleep he started the process all over again. He treated himself to a beer on Friday nights at the jazz club. Saturday was for laundry and food shopping, and he studied all day Sunday. The tooth of the week was the maxillary left first bicuspid. His soap dish contained incisors already graded. The dissection of the arm was nearly complete, and because of the time they spent with him, they named their cadaver. 'Charlie' was the most important member of the anatomy group. They spent many hours with Charlie and were discovering all of his internal secrets.

Anthony expected Amy to be popular in dental school but never imagined it would be because of her glass coffee table. The dental anatomy drawings could be traced through the glass instead of measuring and doing freehand drawings. It may have been unethical, but many students did it to save time. Because Anthony knew that Amy's generosity usually involved a price tag, he continued to hand in his less-than-ideal freehand drawings. He expected he would get a C regardless of what he handed in, as C was the standard grade given to the back-row students. The front-row students were graded generously, and the grading seemed suspicious to the back row. One day Ron Zee traded his bicuspid carvings with Steve Asher. They waited to see what grade the teacher would assign. As expected, Ron got his usual C even though it was Steve's work, and Steve got an A. After that, the back row knew they were screwed. They decided to keep a low profile and accept their mediocre grades.

***

Anna and Rebecca, as senior dental students, spent most of the day treating patients on the clinic floor. Anna started the morning with her usual rant about the dental smocks for the girls in the clinic. "Why do the men get normal-looking blazers and we have to wear these ridiculous smocks?"

"You just don't understand the fashion statement the school administration is trying to make," teased Rebecca.

"I think the statement is that they don't know what to do with women in the dental school and feel the need to hide their bodies."

"You know," sighed Rebecca, "I don't understand why we can't wear blazers. They are not revealing. These garments look like smocks for art class." The smocks had puffy three-quarter sleeves, zipped in the front, and fit loosely above the breast to hide any hint of a female shape. The garments were made of unbreathable polyester material and did not have convenient pockets like the men's blazers. Rebecca felt they had to choose their battles, and the smocks were unimportant. If they complained too much, the older instructors would question the wisdom of admitting women to dental school.

Rebecca started the day with a new patient, a guy her age.

"Blake Cooper."

He stood up, and before her eyes was the most perfect specimen of a man she had ever seen. He was tall and muscular with black hair, blue eyes, a neat mustache, and a face that was so handsome he attracted attention. As she moved close to him, he even smelled good. She thought to herself, *why me?* She already had to act like a licensed dentist even though she was only a student, and now she had to act as a professional and treat this gorgeous hunk like any other patient.

"Hello Blake, I'm Dr. Monahan. We can discuss any concerns you may have after a review of your medical history. Then we will take a full set of X-rays and discuss your treatment."

Blake was by far the most handsome man she had ever met. He was already attracting attention; the hygienists were suddenly hanging around the diagnosis department. The woman in charge of X-rays gave Rebecca far more assistance than was necessary, and the behavior of her female colleagues embarrassed Rebecca. The crazy thing was that Blake seemed oblivious to his effect on women. He was a nice guy, almost shy, and Rebecca was determined to subdue her admiration and focus on his teeth. After all, nobody's perfect. He had a cavity. After finishing his hygiene appointment, she scheduled him for the filling.

Anna approached Rebecca in the hygiene department. "Oh my God, Becca, who was that guy?"

"His name is Blake, and he's very nice; he will be my patient next week for a restoration. I am afraid I will have to threaten his admirers with my high speed."

Anna smiled. "It's fortunate they assigned him to you, Rebecca. His appearance might threaten a male student."

Rebecca did not have a response to that. She felt threatened by his appearance. She never considered how awkward it would be to work with a patient she found attractive. Rebecca knew how to proceed with his work, she had to look past him and concentrate on his teeth. She knew she could do it.

Rebecca had Operative block for the rest of the afternoon. She dreaded it, the rotation where fillings were done. She recognized the need to improve her skills. Each preparation required a certain retention form so the filling would not dislodge, and decay had to be removed to preserve tooth structure. Silver fillings were used for posterior teeth, and acid-etched bonded restorations were placed in the anterior.

Two instructors graded the work done in Operative block, and both were demanding and unsympathetic. Dr. Sherman didn't like Rebecca because she was a woman and her work was not improving. Dr. Cavit was less biased; he just criticized her work. She tried to follow their suggestions, but the negativity was affecting her performance. When she asked for help, she expected them to be more supportive for the sake of her patients. Dr. Sherman was dismissive and would not assist her. After a frustrating afternoon, she left the clinic floor and fought back tears until she returned to the safety of her apartment. After a quick dinner and a bit of self-pity, she drove back to the school to continue Dr. Bloom's lecture notes. The clinic was closed as she made her way to the third floor. She welcomed the project Dr. Bloom had left for her since she needed to get her mind off her disastrous day in the clinic. The only sounds on the third floor were the opening and closing of doors and vacuuming.

Pinkish was working alone that night. Anthony left early because the cafeteria coffee upset his stomach. Pinkish walked into the office when Rebecca was deep in thought.

"Excuse me, Miss."

He started emptying the trash bins. Rebecca handed him the one under her desk. He gave her a concerned look. "Are you sad, Miss?" Rebecca had been crying.

"I'm fine, but thank you for asking. Do you work here every night?"

"Yes, until 7. How about you?"

"I come in when I have assignments. I usually stay until 7 o'clock. I'm Rebecca."

"Pinkish."

She could tell by his accent and hesitation that English was not his first language. Maybe India? She was curious about the custodial staff since she would be on the floor with them. "Do you work alone?"

"No, my accomplice is not here tonight. He stays until 7 o'clock too."

The other custodian must be the voice, thought Rebecca. Pinkish would not be able to sing without an accent.

"Does your accomplice sing?"

"Oh yes, beautiful voice. I am thinking I should record him."

The mystery was solved: the voice belonged to the other janitor. "Pleased to meet you, Pinkish."

Rebecca felt more comfortable working after hours. She was glad she had met Pinkish and looked forward to music and possibly a serenade when she returned. At 7 pm she headed to her car. When she arrived at her apartment, she decided to treat herself to a relaxing soak in the clawfoot tub because the day had been exhausting and she needed to decompress.

Chapter 10

Anthony's anatomy group finished dissecting the arm. The lab practical was on Monday, which left them two days for review. They panicked when they realized some of the cadavers had anatomy that differed from the diagrams in the workbook. The students should have been studying all thirteen cadavers instead of concentrating only on their specimens. Anthony had a sinking feeling about Monday's test and suspected Dr. Hall was enjoying the chaos as they took one last look at the dissections during class. Pinkish and Anthony planned to sneak in some study during working hours and headed to the anatomy lab after finishing their janitorial tasks on the third floor.

That night, Rebecca was on the third floor revising notes on light-cure composites. Light curing was a recent advancement, and she was so engrossed in the lecture notes that she at first failed to notice Mia and Dr. Hall lingering in the office. She wondered why they hadn't left; they were usually gone by 5 pm. Determined to concentrate on her work, she tried to shake the feeling they were waiting for her to leave. Though she did not like Dr. Hall, she could see how some women might find him attractive. He was in his thirties and had an intellectual look with his dark beard and piercing dark eyes. She hoped they would have the common sense to avoid a physical relationship; Dr. Hall was a married man.

At 7 pm she left and tried to glimpse the second janitor with the voice. She saw a light in the anatomy lab. As she peered in the glass window, she saw the two janitors huddled over a cadaver, looking at a dissected arm. She turned and hurried down the hall, upset by what she had seen. She didn't want to know what Dr. Hall, Mia, or the two janitors were doing; it was none of her business.

"Are we supposed to be doing this?" asked Pinkish.

"Probably not," said Anthony, "but do you think they would kick us out of school for studying? I'm sure Dr. Hall knows we are in here. As far as I know, he hasn't left."

"We are doomed," Pinkish lamented with a defeated nod.

***

Ellen and Rebecca headed to the laundromat on Saturday night and had fun while accomplishing everyday mundane tasks together. They talked about their careers and plans for the future. Ellen suggested they stop thinking about what would happen next year, as they were both undecided about their paths moving forward.

"We need to have fun, Rebecca. Come with me to a Halloween party on Wednesday."

" I never go out in the middle of the week. Why didn't they have the party tonight?"

"It's a tradition to have it on Halloween night. Four guys in my medical school class have had a party every year, and this will be the last one since we will graduate and have residencies next fall."

"Do you want me to go? I don't have a costume."

"That's part of the fun. We can go to the consignment shop tomorrow afternoon. They have costume rentals. We don't have to linger at the party; I know you have clinic on Thursday morning. The party is a blast because everyone tries to hide their identity."

Rebecca doubted she could hide her identity with her red hair, but she didn't know too many medical students. "I'll do it for you, Ellen. I suppose now that we are adults there won't be many more Halloween parties."

Sunday was a beautiful fall day, sunny, but brisk. Walking to the consignment shop was a fun adventure. The rental costumes from Friday and Saturday were already being returned, so a wide selection was available. Ellen rented a Raggedy Ann costume. Rebecca was struggling to find an outfit when the shopkeeper looked at Rebecca's red hair and had a brilliant idea.

"I have the perfect costume for you," she exclaimed. She rummaged through the inventory and brought it out.

Rebecca laughed. "Oh ... I can't."

"Just try it on; if you don't like it, you can choose something else."

Rebecca emerged from the dressing room in a mermaid costume. It was ridiculous and sexy at the same time. She had a sparkly crown, a dress with a fitted bodice and pencil skirt. Green sequins adorned the costume, and a long slit ran up the side so she could walk.

Ellen was laughing too. "It's perfect, Rebecca, you have to take it."

"It would be fun to wear it. I don't know many medical students, so they won't know who I am anyway."

***

On Monday morning, the freshman class was anxious. Dr. Hall gave the lab practical in shifts because only thirteen students could take it at the same time. The schedule for the day was atypical, since the microbiology exam was given on the same day. Anthony took the microbiology test in the morning and took the lab practical in the afternoon. Anthony, Joe, Pinkish, Amy, Ron, and Roy stood in the hallway outside the anatomy lab waiting for their turn. The previous group looked distraught when they left the testing area. The comments were alarming.

"Unfair!"

"Good luck! You'll need it."

"What a bastard!"

"I had no idea what I was doing."

They were being set up for failure. When Anthony started the test, he knew the intent was to trick them. Some structures were difficult to see, and the students were not permitted to touch the cadavers. The blood vessels were twisted purposefully before they were pinned. Dr. Hall included anomalies wherever he could. They all left the anatomy lab praying for a passing grade. At 5 pm, Anthony and Pinkish were in the elevator with their cleaning carts, headed for the third floor. They went through the motions with heavy hearts.

"We are threaded."

"The term is screwed!"

"Yes, that too."

They finished their third-floor tasks in a stupor and left a few minutes early. Anthony crashed as soon as he got home; he didn't even make his bed. He had another test in the morning, but sleep had become more important than a last-minute review. The week was disastrous, but by Wednesday he felt more rested. On Halloween, he had classes during the day, but Jeff gave the custodial crew the night off. Anthony was happy to hand candy out to kids in the neighborhood but had to subdue Ralphie's eager excitement when the doorbell rang. Chuck was getting ready for a party thrown by the medical students who lived next door. Chuck dressed up as Zorro.

"Hey Tony, lights out at 8:30; we have a party to go to."

"I'm staying home, Chuck. I don't know the medical students and don't have a costume."

"You're invited, Tony. You don't want to seem stuck-up."

"I'm sure I won't be missed."

"Come on, will we ever go to a party together? I can go because the business is closed tonight. The jazz club had parties over the weekend."

"I don't like Halloween, Chuck."

Anthony looked at the disappointment on Chuck's face. "I'll tell you what. If you have a costume I can hide behind, I will go with you."

Moments later, Chuck appeared with a pirate hat, a rubber sword, an eyepatch, and a large gold earring. "Here you go. Put on a white shirt and jeans. I will wait for you to get dressed."

"And how do you propose I wear that eyepatch over my glasses?"

"Come on, Tony, are you so nearsighted you can't walk next door without your glasses? Put the patch over your bad eye."

"I am nearsighted in both eyes, Chuck."

"Whatever. The medical students will invite plenty of nurses to the party. It's about time that you get out, and stop acting like a monk."

Chuck was persistent, but maybe he was right. After those tests, Anthony needed a beer. Reluctantly, he put on the earring, hat, and eye patch, but refused to bring the rubber sword. The party was in full swing by the time they arrived. They walked through the back door and into the kitchen to get a beer. The partygoers Anthony spoke to remained incognito, so he wasn't sure if he knew them. The first beer went down easily. He grabbed a second beer and wandered into the living room. He stopped short when he saw the red-haired mermaid. Her costume was amusing, but somehow sexy too. He was certain she wouldn't recognize him, especially without glasses and with a patch over one eye. The guy next to him told a ridiculous joke, and he had to smile.

Rebecca looked at the pirate and recognized him when he smiled. The dimples, the easy smile, the exquisitely shaped teeth. He was the one who walked her home from the jazz club. She had hoped she would meet him again. He looked like a pirate; his dark brown hair was longer than she remembered, and rolled-up sleeves displayed strong, muscular arms. He was wearing a large gold earring. His shirt was open, he was unshaven, and he had a powerful look, a primitive, dangerous look. He appeared even more attractive than she remembered. She must approach him tonight. It was Halloween after all, and she could be as forward as she wanted to be. She walked over to him and took his hand. He obediently followed her onto the porch.

"I'm sorry; it was loud in there, and I wanted to talk to you."

"Whaaat?"

She smiled at his ridiculous joke.

The night was chilly, but Anthony did not feel the cold. At first, he was tongue-tied, but then he remembered he was a fearless pirate.

"Have you come to lure me into the sea?"

For a few moments, Rebecca was speechless. That voice—the janitor! She calmed herself and tried to play along.

"Yes, I've been watching you, and you're my next quarry."

"Interesting, but unfortunate. The closest ocean is 1300 miles away."

"Oh, I think I can still entice you to come with me."

"Perhaps, but in the meantime, you are alone on the porch with a dangerous pirate. In this landlocked situation, you should be concerned."

Rebecca couldn't help herself. She started to giggle.

"You mock me at your own peril," he said with a rakish grin.

"I'm not afraid of you, sir. You don't have a weapon."

"But I do," he whispered. "It's hidden."

She felt the blush rise in her cheeks. "Do you recall meeting me in the past?" she asked.

"How could I forget?"

"Do you remember everything?"

"I do," he replied softly. "Do you?"

Rebecca grasped him and gazed into his eye. She had to find out if the spark she felt that night was real or her drunken memory. She leaned into him.

The intensity of his desire dazed him. "May I?"

She had to smile that this dangerous plunderer had asked permission. Rebecca went to him as his strong, gentle arms wrapped around her. They got lost in a steamy kiss. It was not a spark she felt; it was an inferno, exhilarating and overwhelming. Heat rushed through as they got lost in each other's arms. The sound of the front door opening caused them to pause. Ellen was coming onto the porch.

"Oh, I'm sorry."

"Ellen, I was just looking for you."

Ellen gave Rebecca an incredulous look. "You were?"

"You know I have an early morning, Ellen."

"Right." Ellen turned. "I'll get our coats."

Rebecca thought her coat was the last thing she needed. She was burning.

Anthony loosened his hold on her. "When can I see you again?"

She shot him a playful grin. "I guess it will be on the third floor."

He was speechless. She knew. She kissed him even though she was aware of his menial job. Most of the women here were looking for a doctor. The girls smiled at him as they walked down the steps. He removed the eyepatch so he would get a better view of them as they walked down the street. Just then the front door opened; Chuck.

"Way to go, Tony," he said sarcastically.

"What now, Chuck?"

"I waited all night for a chance to meet Raggedy Ann. When she finally broke loose from her admirers, I was ready to make a move, but she walked in on you ravishing the mermaid."

"Were you spying on us, Chuck?"

"You should be thankful I was the one standing by the window. You two would have attracted a crowd."

Anthony was getting mad at Chuck. The kiss was an intimate moment. He assumed privacy when he was on the porch with Rebecca.

"Just a word of advice, Tony. I spoke to Rebecca that night at the club. I think your Little Mermaid has had bad luck with men. She's a girl who needs to take it slow. What were you thinking? You weren't even on a date!"

He was furious. "She didn't seem to mind!"

"Tony, she was just being polite."

Anthony thought Rebecca was the politest girl he had ever met. "I'm going home now, Chuck."

"Good, 'cause I'm going back in to get drunk."

Anthony was angry, but Chuck had a point. What was he thinking? That was the second time he had kissed her without even asking her out. He should be ashamed of himself. He let Ralphie out and then went upstairs to take a shower ... a cold one.

Ellen asked questions when they were a few houses away from the party. "Would you like to tell me what just happened?"

"That was the guy, Ellen. The one that walked me home from the jazz club."

"Oh good. Did you find out anything else about him?"

"He's the voice, the janitor."

"Rebecca, you're not making any sense. You're beginning to sound like Goldie Hawn in that movie with Chevy Chase. Have you seen it?"

"No, is it good?"

"Never mind," said Ellen. "What is this about a voice?"

"The guy who walked me home from the jazz club and the guy who cleans the third-floor offices are one and the same. I didn't make the connection until tonight."

"You think he's a janitor?"

"I don't know; it's so confusing. Why was he at the medical school Halloween party?"

"Good point."

"Anyway, the first time he kissed me..."

"Wait, I think I missed something."

"I was embarrassed, so I didn't tell you I kissed him the night he walked me home from the jazz club."

"So you kissed him again?"

"Right."

"So how was it?"

"Ellen, the reason I had to leave at that moment is that I was afraid if I didn't he would end up in my bed."

"Rebecca, I never heard you say anything like that!"

"I have never said anything like that before."

Ellen paused thoughtfully, and tried to evaluate the situation.

"This isn't a rebound thing because of Kyle, is it?"

"Kyle who?"

"Not Kyle. You're not reading those romance novels. You know that life isn't like that."

"I read *Pride and Prejudice* in high school. Is that a romance novel?"

"So it's not that. What then?"

Rebecca paused and contemplated the question. "It's hard to explain, Ellen; it's biological, like natural selection. There is something about his smile, his voice, even his scent that enticed me; I'm sure it was only soap, but it reminded me of my dad's Old Spice. It's like a primal instinct telling me to choose this one."

"Well, Rebecca, I suggest you find out more about this guy before you follow your intuition, though I admit he's definitely cute."

Chapter 11

November 1st was a bitter, wintry day with snow flurries. Rebecca was fighting fatigue because of a restless night thinking about Anthony. She still knew very little about him. After her classes in the morning, she saw two patients in the afternoon, a denture patient, and an emergency. She was determined to focus on these appointments. Mrs. Murray was her denture patient. She had extractions and a temporary denture; treated by a senior who had graduated last year. The denture did not fit because of shrinkage at the extraction sites, and the patient had also lost weight. The student placed a soft lining in the denture so the patient could wear it while these changes took place. Rebecca was the new dentist assigned to the case, and the treatment plan was to fabricate a new upper denture. Rebecca introduced herself.

"Good afternoon, Mrs. Murray, I'm Dr. Monahan. I'd like to review your medical history before we start treatment. Have there been any changes since last spring?" Rebecca went through the long questionnaire. The patient told her that the only medication she was taking was Tylenol. She also had an allergy to penicillin. Rebecca then fitted impression trays and measured the alginate she would need to take the impressions. Afterward, she would pour up a stone model and fabricate custom trays to take the final impression. At the end of the appointment, the patient had a request.

"Dr. Monahan, can you prescribe a medicine for pain?"

"Where is your pain?" asked Rebecca. "Is a lower tooth bothering you?"

"No," she replied, "it's the denture that hurts."

"Maybe I can adjust it and replace the lining."

"No thanks," said Mrs. Murray. "I think I just need pain medicine."

Despite her limited experience with patients, Rebecca saw a red flag. She wondered how she should handle this. "Mrs. Murray, I'm sure you're aware I'm a student. I am not licensed to prescribe without instructor approval."

"But the last doctor gave me pills." She sighed. "Never mind, I'll just take Tylenol."

The patient looked defeated, and Rebecca was astounded. She never would have expected this patient would ask for opioids. She wondered if the student gave her medication from the dispensary, but did not want to speculate.

Her second patient was in pain and couldn't wait for his appointment. He had a 'hot tooth' sensitive to everything. Rebecca knew adequate anesthesia was the first hurdle. She administered her mandibular block injection until the patient had profound numbness of his tongue and lip on the left side. Immediate relief was apparent. Rebecca was tentative about placing the rubber dam and starting the root canal. She repeated, "If you feel anything at all, let me know." The lidocaine worked like magic, and the patient fell asleep during the procedure. He was probably exhausted from being up all night. Rebecca was getting bleary-eyed herself but disinfected the canals and placed a sedative medication in the tooth so she could finish the root canal at the next visit. Rebecca left the clinic early and went home. She attended evening Mass since it was All Saints' Day, and by 9 pm she was in bed and sleeping soundly.

***

On Friday afternoon, the freshmen received their lab practical grades. The entire class was distraught, and very few passed. Anthony couldn't believe his 48% but in a way he expected it. He would need a near-perfect score on the next lab practical to get a C in the course. He left the first-floor lab in disgust and forgot to take his lecture notes with him.

Rebecca hoped she might run into Anthony. She walked to the school's lower level to get coffee; she was still tired from her busy week. On the way, she passed the freshman lab and noticed a pretty blond girl alone in the room. She was crying. Rebecca's instinct was to go talk to her, but then she held back, remembering her oath to Anna that they would not cry in front of their colleagues.

A few minutes later, Anthony returned to the lab to get his notes. Amy was there, crying. "What's wrong, Amy?" he asked.

Amy stood up when she saw him. "Anthony, I don't know how I am going to get through this year." She showed him her lab practical grade—65%.

"Not bad," remarked Anthony. "Since it's a D, you can bring up your grade."

" I feel like such a failure." She walked forward and stood in front of him, sobbing into his chest.

He instinctively wrapped his arms around her to comfort her. "Don't worry, we all got lousy grades. Dr. Hall might have to grade on a curve."

"Oh no, I heard he never curves his tests."

At that moment, Rebecca peeked into the freshman lab and witnessed the embrace. She couldn't believe Anthony was in the freshman lab. The blond girl was weeping in his arms, and the scene looked intimate and personal. Rebecca wondered if Anthony was responsible for the tears, and she suspected he was just another heartbreaker, another poor choice. She tried to step away unnoticed. When she headed towards the stairs, she heard a familiar voice calling her name.

"Rebecca!"

She turned, and as she did, she realized she had her name tag on. Anthony approached and read it in disbelief.

"Dr. Monahan?"

"Guilty as charged. And to whom am I speaking?"

"Anthony Roselli."

"Can I assume you're a student here?"

"A freshman."

They stood in silence. After a pause, Rebecca stood with her hands on her chest, looking him over deliberately.

"I didn't realize they were requiring the freshmen to be janitors."

"I assure you, it's voluntary. My lab partner, Pinkish, is also working as a custodian."

Rebecca didn't know what to say. She decided on an aloof, professional response. " I wish you the best of luck, Anthony. Freshman year can be very challenging."

And before Anthony could say another word, she took off. She dumped her lousy coffee and decided to go home.

Anthony was stunned. He never met a girl who could be so steamy hot and so icy cold. Chuck was right; he had been too forward and offended her. He didn't understand this uncontrollable desire to be with her. It must be biology; he was hopelessly attracted. Where was his reserved and level-headed self? Then his reality set in. Who was he kidding? Anthony could dream about her, but what did he have to offer? He had no money, no time, and his career was on hold for the next four years. He was younger and had less experience with women than most guys his age. The last thing he needed was a woman to complicate his life. And not any woman, but one who could be as fiery as a volcano or as cold as an iceberg. Still, he regretted how this had all played out. He had her phone number and should have called the day after the jazz club incident. Now it was too late. All he could hope for was a friendly hello and the privilege of admiring her from afar.

Chapter 12

November was a dreary month. Many students went home for Thanksgiving weekend, but since Rebecca was from New Jersey, Anna from California, and Ellen from Montana, the girls planned to stay in town and celebrate the holiday in Rebecca's apartment. Rebecca dismissed all thoughts of Anthony; though she could have misinterpreted what she saw in the freshman lab, the prospect of getting involved with him seemed hopeless from the start. She knew what it was like to be a first-year dental student, and because of the enormous workload freshman year, there was very little time to nurture a relationship, and best to avoid entanglements. The proof was in the two students in her class who had gotten divorced, and with her friend Ellen and her broken engagement.

Dental materials articles were pouring in from various sources, and Rebecca admired the practitioners who shared their thoughts and findings to promote better dentistry. She heard music in the hallways while she worked but did not hear or see Anthony for several weeks. Rebecca had to smile when she thought about their encounter on the porch; much like a scene from a movie, an unforgettable one.

Dr. Hall and Mia were again spending time together after hours, and Rebecca was certain something was going on between them. Rebecca would have considered bringing work home with her so she wouldn't be a witness to their indiscretions, but Dr. Bloom insisted the information stay in the office.

***

Pinkish and Anthony had become efficient in their maintenance duties, able to complete them in record time, except that night when Anthony had a mishap. He was steering the janitor's cart toward the restrooms when he looked into the office and saw Rebecca. She had a strange power over him, and he could not take his eyes off her. He felt an intense longing and loneliness that surprised him since their encounters had been brief and they hadn't dated. Suddenly, the reality of Dr. Hall's annoyed gaze jolted him to attention. As Anthony turned, he knocked the entire cart over on its side. Now he had everyone's attention. Rebecca looked at him, then smiled, and he seemed so embarrassed she felt sorry for him.

Dr. Hall confronted him in the hallway. "Is there something I can help you with, Mr. Roselli?"

"No, Dr. Hall, I'm sorry to disturb you."

"I know who you're looking at, and you might as well forget it."

"I don't know what you're talking about, sir."

"You should concentrate on your studies. I would say you're the student most likely to flunk out."

"I would hate to deprive you of my company, Dr. Hall. I'm sure I can pass for your sake."

Dr. Hall returned to the office, but Rebecca was there and heard the entire exchange. She felt an unexplained longing and a desire to protect Anthony from Dr. Hall. She wanted to help him and imagined they could be friends.

Anthony's clumsiness mortified him. *Real smooth,* he groaned to himself. Not only did he humiliate himself in front of Rebecca, he was now an adversary to Dr. Hall, who seemed to allow his personal feelings to influence final grades. Even if he could pass anatomy this semester, he would have Dr. Hall for neuroanatomy and head and neck anatomy next semester. He hoped his upper-class tutor would help him raise his grade to a C. The dental school administration did not want students to flunk out, so the ones in academic trouble were given extra help, and Anthony was one of those students. The freshman class now banded together while in anatomy lab, and this time they studied all the cadavers before taking the lab practical. The guys in Anthony's group could not bring themselves to dissect Charlie's male organs, so they asked Amy to do the job. Charlie was well-studied since he was the only male cadaver in the anatomy lab.

***

Rebecca left school early before the break. She didn't blame the last patient for canceling. He must have decided routine fillings the day before Thanksgiving was a bad idea. She was thinking about Thanksgiving preparations as she entered her apartment later that afternoon. She was in the habit of locking the door as soon as she entered. A few minutes later she heard a knock on the door, and she couldn't imagine who it could be. As she looked through the glass window of the kitchen door, she saw an unfamiliar man at her door; he was wearing a scarf around his face.

"I'm here to check the electric meter in your apartment," he said.

"You'll have to talk to the landlord next door," she replied.

The man motioned that he couldn't hear her through the door. She wouldn't open the door to him, but he could have forced it open. Her heart started pounding as she experienced a sense of impending danger. She wedged a kitchen chair in the door and dialed Ellen on the phone.

"Ellen, there is a man on my landing, and I am afraid. Look out your window and call the police if he tries to break in."

Donna and Ellen ignored Rebecca's orders and walked onto their landing. When the man saw them, he descended the steps and ran down the road. Afterward, the girls met in her kitchen as Rebecca tried to calm herself.

"Thank God we were home," sighed Donna.

"Did you recognize him?" asked Ellen.

"No, but he must have been watching me as I entered my apartment."

"Should we call the police?" Donna asked, shaken.

"What would I say? I couldn't see his face, and he didn't commit a crime. The police can't arrest him for intent."

All three girls were upset. When they told Mrs. Capalini what had happened, she immediately called a locksmith, who installed deadbolts. The girls insisted Mrs. Capalini include her apartment since she was a senior citizen living alone.

***

Anthony drove to his parents' house for Thanksgiving and the weekend. His sister Angela was chatty about her first semester at college and had some amusing stories to tell. Tommy informed Anthony that he planned to pop the question to his steady girlfriend on Christmas Eve; he could see how much his brother loved Julie and was happy for them. His parents adjusted to their empty nest and seemed content. He hated to discuss problems at dental school, but his family sensed he was having a hard time, and his mother told him she was saying the rosary for him every day. He thanked God when he got into dental school; now he should pray that he could stay in. Two classmates had already dropped out, but Anthony was determined to rise above the challenges and follow his dreams.

Chapter 13

By the middle of December, the freshmen had finished their dental anatomy drawings and carvings, the last tooth being the mandibular left second molar. The third molars, known as wisdom teeth, were too irregular to study their anatomy. The class was preparing for the finals week, a pivotal time in their journey as many students dropped out or flunked out after one semester. As they sat in the lecture hall, they were told the microbiology teacher, Dr. Staab, had remarks about the progress of the class.

"I hope the entire class is here," he started, "because you all need to hear this. At least half of you are in danger academically. Since it seems like I have to spoon-feed you to finish this microbiology course, I am handing out an outline of the topics on the final exam. Be aware there will be no trick questions, and it will be multiple choice. If you don't get a passing grade, I assume you did not study. Some of you need a perfect score on the final to pass the course. Good luck. This is my fourth year at the dental school, and I must say you are either the laziest or the least talented group of students I have had to teach. Dentistry is a tough profession and is not for the faint of heart. You should search your soul to determine if it is right for you. It is your life and your decision and we would not criticize you for changing course.

If you need help with microbiology, I will be in my office during lunch and I can stay until 5 pm for anyone who needs extra help. Now the dean has closing remarks."

The dean started towards the front of the classroom and looked around. He was addressing the wrong group of students. He instead went to the back of the room and stood directly in front of Anthony and Pinkish.

"First of all," said the dean, "I want you to know my office is open to you and we can talk about any problem you wish to discuss." He paused and took a look around the classroom. "You have been a challenging group of students. I still have confidence that most of you will become dentists. In temperament and appearance, you are outliers in the profession, and I don't expect Crest or Colgate to hire you for their commercials. That being said, diversity of thought and diversity of life experience can be a good thing. Some of you could become involved in research; others may be just different enough to attract patients who could otherwise avoid dental care. I want you to pass, but no one will hold your hand. It doesn't matter who you are or where you're from; if you complete the next 3 1/2 years of study, you will be a competent practitioner. One concern of your professors is the rumor that some students have been tracing the dental anatomy drawings. I have to tell you I am disappointed. You may not see the logic in the projects we require, but the exercise is valuable. We assigned the drawings and carvings to help you develop the motor skills and precision you will need for dentistry, not to give you interesting additions to your soap dish."

He heard a chuckle from the group. "In addition, we will enforce a dress code next semester. Men must wear socks, no flip-flops or clogs, and your hair and facial foliage should be trimmed. I must commend the women in this class for their ability to dress professionally, so please continue to do so. I understand some of you wear makeup to hide that tired look among students. Please keep it to a minimum. When you get up to the clinic floor, the men will wear ties, and the women, slacks. No jeans, no exceptions. Believe it or not, I remember what it was like to be a dental student. Some of your instructors are very demanding, but there is a reason; your patients will expect excellence, and why shouldn't they? There is great responsibility with a dental degree, and it starts during your training. Best of luck to all of you. I hope to see you next semester and look forward to shaking your hand on the podium in May 1983."

Dean Gallagher and Dr. Staab then left the classroom. It was so quiet, you could hear a pin drop. The students began to exit the room, but Anthony and Pinkish had to wait for their third-floor shift.

***

Rebecca had not seen Judy or Mia for over a week. She was alone in the office with Dr. Hall and tried to ignore him. She breathed a sigh of relief when he left, only to become distressed when he returned a short time later. He was staring at her. Finally, she confronted him.

"Is there something I can help you with, Dr. Hall?"

"I wondered if you would be interested in doing work for me. Mia is taking a leave of absence."

"Oh, I'm sorry to hear that. Is she sick?"

"No, she has a family problem."

"I appreciate the offer, but I am busy with Dr. Bloom's lectures. I really can't manage any more hours."

She stood up to get copy paper from the cabinet, and Dr. Hall was right behind her. When she turned, he was standing very close to her, and she felt boxed in. For a moment she shrank from the piercing gaze of the anatomy instructor like she did when she was a freshman.

Anthony looked into the third-floor office and saw Dr. Hall and Rebecca in the corner. Rebecca looked vulnerable. His overwhelming instinct was to protect her. He grabbed his weapon of choice and stepped into the office with it. He turned it on. The vacuum created a diversion as Rebecca slipped past Dr. Hall as she grabbed her purse.

"I just remembered I have an appointment I have to keep." She escaped and gave Anthony a grateful smile. He was left to face the wrath of Dr. Hall.

"Mr. Roselli, you have become an annoyance," commented the professor.

"Just doing my job, sir."

" You are skilled at maintenance. I'm glad you have a backup plan since I don't expect you to be around next year."

Anthony stood up straight and glared at his adversary. He was younger, in better shape, and three inches taller. But being reserved and a master of self-control, he disregarded his desire to confront Dr. Hall and braced himself for the verbal assault that was sure to follow.

"Poor Mr. Roselli. I'm sure you won't get the degree or the girl."

Anthony turned on the vacuum to discourage further discussion. Pinkish walked by and gave him a wide-eyed, concerned look. Dr. Hall departed soon afterward, and as Anthony finished his shift he tried to look forward to his weekend.

***

The third-floor music was blaring as usual on Monday afternoon, and Dr. Hall was nowhere to be found. Rebecca was grading tests for

Dr. Bloom when she noticed Anthony walking past. She ran into the hallway to meet him. "Anthony, do you have a minute?"

"Of course. Is there something you need for the office?"

"No, I just wanted to thank you for your intervention on Friday. I am so sorry it may have put you in a precarious position with Dr. Hall. He's one to hold a grudge."

He flashed her a smile. "I was already on his naughty list. I doubt it made any difference."

Rebecca appreciated Anthony; he was gallant and funny. "Listen, I would like to return the favor. I don't know if this will help, but I found my freshman-year lab practical. It could give you an idea of the structures he might tag."

He took the test paper. "98%. I'm impressed."

"Don't be, the truth is I got a 46% when I studied the arm. This near-perfect score brought my final grade to a C."

"Sounds like my plan of action. Thanks."

Rebecca suddenly felt that the offering wasn't enough. She touched his arm to project warmth and sincerity. She wondered if this simple gesture affected him the way it did her. "I saved all my notes from freshman year. You are welcome to anything, all you have to do is ask."

"Anything?" he whispered with a smoldering smile.

Her eyes sparkled with amusement as she turned back to her work. She wanted their role-playing to continue. Anthony was still a fearless, sexy pirate, and he rescued her once again.

Chapter 14

The students spent exam week studying and completing requirements. Freshmen and sophomores studied every moment; at breakfast, lunch, and dinner, in bed, and even in the bathtub. Anthony fell asleep on his notes and hoped he would somehow assimilate the material. Pinkish and Anthony quizzed each other whenever they were working side by side.

Pinkish witnessed the incident with Dr. Hall, Rebecca, and Anthony. He was concerned about his friend and was sensitive to his feelings. Although he did not understand or approve of how Americans found their partners, he noticed Anthony's affinity for Rebecca and the friction between him and Dr. Hall. In his country, parents arranged the marriage. Although Americans found this concept archaic, it usually worked well, especially if two loving families were involved. He had fond thoughts of Ira, a girl from his neighborhood who was studying in India. Ira was his promised one. They grew up together, though Pinkish was three years older. When the families proposed a marriage arrangement, Pinkish thought Ira was just as happy as he was. They had a deepening awareness of each other when they were teenagers and started seeing each other in their 20s. The plan was to get married and live in America, but if immigration presented a problem, Pinkish would return to India to be her husband.

Anthony looked at Rebecca the same way Pinkish looked at Ira. He realized Anthony would become Rebecca's friend if they saw each other every day. Pinkish devised a plan for Anthony.

"Tony, I do not like my third-floor assignment," he complained. "I do not want to interact with Dr. Hall. Would you trade?"

"Are you sure?" he asked. "Cleaning the anatomy lab instead of the office is a step in the wrong direction."

" I do not know about direction, but I do not want to converse with Dr. Hall."

"If that's what you want," agreed Anthony, "we can switch tonight."

A daily ritual started between Anthony and Rebecca when he entered the office to clean. She spent more time on her makeup and hair because of it, and for Anthony it was the best part of his day. Rebecca was at the office every day. Christmas was on a Tuesday, and the last day for most students was the Thursday before Christmas. After his final exams, Anthony searched for Rebecca on the third floor.

"Hi, Rebecca. I want to wish you a Merry Christmas. I'm leaving in the morning."

"Merry Christmas, Anthony. Enjoy your family and get some rest."

He stood there gazing at her and seemed emotional. He longed to kiss her goodbye but tried to be satisfied with the sparkling smile she had for him. "Rebecca, I don't know if I will see you next semester."

She was deeply concerned. "Are you dropping out?"

"No, but I am worried about my grades. I did my best, but I am afraid it might not be good enough."

Rebecca stood up and took his hand in hers. "I thought I was going to flunk out freshman year, and here I am, one semester away from graduation. I have confidence that you will be here three years from now."

"I hope you're right," he answered. "But in case things don't work out, I want you to know how much I admire you. Our friendship has been the highlight of this adventure, and I will always remember it. Merry Christmas, Rebecca."

He handed her a card with a small box and a handwritten note: '*So you may never forget how we both love the sea.*'

This thoughtful gesture moved her, but the prospect of not seeing him again distressed her. When she opened the box, it contained a keychain. It had a mermaid charm and was from Seaside Heights, New Jersey.

"Anthony, this is surprising; how did you get this?"

"I'll just say I know a guy."

"My keychain tends to break."

"I noticed," he replied with a sad smile.

Instinctively, she put her arms around him and hugged him. They held onto each other, neither attempting to move away. Dr. Bloom walked in and cleared his throat to make them aware of his presence. Rebecca's cheeks turned red, as this was more intimate than a friendly hug.

"Dr. Bloom, this is Anthony Roselli. He's a freshman."

"Pleased to meet you, Anthony. You'll see me in dental materials class next year."

"I hope so, sir; I'm looking forward to it."

They wished each other a Merry Christmas and planned to return rested. Rebecca and Anthony left the next day to spend the holidays with their families.

Chapter 15

Dean Gallagher called John Marlow's office on December 26th and left a message on the answering machine.

'Merry Christmas, this is Dean Gallagher. I hope you are having an enjoyable holiday. I'm afraid I need your services again; there was another break-in last Friday. Please call me when you return to the office.'

Mr. Marlow returned the call and met the dean the next day in front of the dental school. The building had been closed.

"It is the same third-floor office," sighed the dean as he led Marlow into the building. "Dr. Bloom notified me immediately when he discovered the condition of the office. He stopped in on Friday afternoon to proofread his newsletter. When he entered the office, it was in complete disarray. I came down immediately and locked the premises. I waited for you to examine the scene."

"Did Dr. Bloom find his notes?" asked Marlow.

"Yes, although someone had rifled through them. They were in a locked drawer, which was opened anyway."

The two men entered the office. The place was a mess.

"Is there valuable research being done at the school?" inquired Marlow.

"Not that I know of. Dr. Bloom is publishing a dental materials newsletter, but all the information will soon be available. Dental research is usually collaborative as most practitioners are generous about sharing their findings."

"How about patents?" asked Marlow. "We should talk to Dr. Bloom and see what he's working on. Are there other professors using this office?"

"Only Dr. Hall, the anatomy instructor. I can't imagine he would be the target."

"What about tests? Could it be students looking for tests?"

"The exams were over on Thursday. A student could want access to change a grade, but it seems unlikely. The only tests stored in this office are in anatomy and dental materials. We have never had a failing grade in Dr. Bloom's class; all the students do well. The anatomy students weren't here last year when the first break-ins occurred."

"I could dust for fingerprints," said Marlow, "but I doubt it will be helpful. I'm sure the perpetrator wore gloves, and even if he didn't, chances are he wouldn't be in a criminal database."

The dean was uncomfortable discussing the next item of concern. "Two employees working in this office quit abruptly before the break. One left without notice and didn't even pick up her last paycheck. The other handed me a letter of resignation."

"What was in the letter?"

"The usual, that she was leaving for a more suitable opportunity. But off the record, a different story."

"What did she say?" asked Marlow.

The dean was hesitant to repeat the conversation.

"Tell me exactly what was said," implored Marlow.

"She said Dr. Hall is a male chauvinist pig and she wouldn't spend another day in the office with him."

"Was that his assistant?"

"No, Mia, his assistant, is the one who left without a word. Judy the hygienist was the one I spoke to."

"That all sounds like a personal conflict," observed Marlow. "I would expect the break-ins could be a separate matter. What about the dispensary?"

"That issue seems to be resolved. All the pain medications were accounted for."

"Were there students working here on Friday?"

"No, the students left on Thursday after exams. I had a professional crew in on Friday to wax the floors."

"I am concerned about the safety of the students working here after hours," said the dean. "I don't want them to be assaulted by an intruder."

Marlow was also concerned about the students. "We have to notify the students of the problem. We will ask for their discretion. I doubt any of them are involved; but I should meet with them when they return and implement a safety protocol."

"Of course," agreed the dean.

"In the meantime, I want the personnel files of everyone who worked on this floor. I must meet with Dr. Bloom and Dr. Hall, and would also like to talk to the three students."

"I will set up a 5 pm meeting with the students the day they return, and will check with Dr. Bloom and Dr. Hall about their availability to meet with you, Mr. Marlow."

"Great. I will look at the personnel files when I come in."

Dean Gallagher seemed distraught. "I thought we had these problems solved. We must get to the bottom of this."

"The key is to find out what they are looking for," said Marlow, "and as far as Dr. Hall is concerned, we won't know what happened unless we get honest answers from the two female employees who quit. Both of them may have reasons to resist being forthcoming."

"Thank you for your assistance, Mr. Marlow. Take your time investigating the premises. I will ask Dr. Bloom and Mrs. Susman to help me get the office in order. Perhaps they will have insight into what happened here."

Chapter 16

Anthony had a fun, relaxing holiday with his family. Tommy and Julie were engaged, and the family shared their joy. Chuck spent his Christmas at the jazz club; a place for customers who liked jazz and did not have family to spend the holidays with. Pinkish spent the day making calls to India and enjoyed listening to the cassettes Anthony gave him as a Christmas gift. That night he went to the jazz club to visit Chuck and the patrons he had become friendly with.

Anthony and Pinkish worked as bartenders for Chuck on New Year's Eve. The business was a success, but Chuck was concerned about a slowdown in January and February when the weather was severe. The atmosphere at the club was welcoming, and it attracted regular customers. As they ushered in the new year, they could enjoy the festivities and avoid being alone.

The three friends all experienced loneliness, though they kept their feelings to themselves. Pinkish missed Ira; they were living on different continents. Anthony dreamed of a woman he couldn't have, and Chuck wanted a steady girlfriend but didn't have one. He was popular with girls as a friend but not as a boyfriend. Chuck was a nice guy who, behind his fun exterior, could also be sensitive and serious.

He was waiting for the right woman whom he could love and who would appreciate him.

***

Rebecca and Anna flew into the airport after the holiday break. They met in the baggage claim area and shared a cab since they lived in the same neighborhood.

"Happy New Year, Rebecca!"

"Hi Anna, how was your break?"

"Wonderful. The temperature was in the 70s. What a cruel reality returning to this place."

As they hailed a cab, a cold wind whipped through their layers of warm clothing.

"I think the air is too cold to breathe."

"I'm going to put a scarf around my face."

"Maybe we shouldn't talk until we get into the cab." The driver was friendly and helped the girls with their luggage. Then they got into the cab, and Rebecca unwrapped the scarf. "Was everything sunny in California?"

"My family survived the holidays without drama. Chris is still waiting for me. He is helping me prepare for my California boards."

Chris was a surfer who financed his passion by being a product representative for a large dental retailer. He met Anna at the California Dental Convention. They had been corresponding for over a year. "I can't believe how devoted he has been. I didn't expect it."

"Don't sell yourself short, Anna; you must be a dream come true: a blonde California girl who loves the beach and is a dentist besides. You could be a power couple in dental circles."

"Maybe," sighed Anna. "I'm not completely sold, but I guess love is growing slowly. His enthusiasm and persistence are hard to resist. But what about you, Rebecca? Did you see Kyle?"

"He called and said he would love to see me. Of course, being his busy season, Kyle didn't ask me on an actual date but invited me to one of his gigs. At first, I told him I couldn't make it, but then I went anyway. I located the table reserved for guests of the band, sat down, and started talking to a girl sitting there. Kyle was on stage, glancing over at both of us. He seemed nervous. During a break, he was obligated to sit down with us and was in the awkward predicament of having the two of us there to see him. He made his choice when he introduced me as an old friend visiting from out of state. I wasn't upset, but so done with him. It was a simple way to end the relationship, and I realized I had no desire to see him again. I finished my drink, said goodbye, and wished them a merry Christmas. He tried to talk to me as I was heading out, but I wouldn't give him a chance. It didn't matter what he said; it was over."

"I wouldn't have been so civil; I might have thrown a drink in his face."

" I was never in love with him; just the idea of him. It was easy to let him go; his first love will always be himself, and I could never be content with that."

The cab dropped Anna off. She shivered when she opened the door of the cab. "I'll see you at school, Rebecca."

Chapter 17

Anthony and Pinkish were apprehensive about Dean Gallagher's request to meet.

"I am thinking we are in great trouble with grades," warned Pinkish. "Maybe they failed to notify us we are terminated."

"If we flunked out, I doubt they would ask to see us together," suggested Anthony. "The rumor is that two students either flunked out or dropped out. They are not here today, but we are. Our grades must have been acceptable."

"Maybe we are probating."

"You mean we are on probation."

"Yes, that's it."

Mrs. Susman led Pinkish and Anthony into the office. Mr. Marlow and Dean Gallagher joined them.

"We are waiting for one more student," noted the dean as they took their seats. "To set your minds at ease, gentlemen, this isn't about grades."

Just then, Rebecca walked in. All being gentlemen, the four men stood.

"Please have a seat. I want to introduce you to Mr. Marlow, a security expert hired by the school. He will explain why you are here and answer questions. Rebecca, are you acquainted with Mr. Roselli and Mr. Singh?"

"Yes, we work on the third floor after school."

All three students looked uneasy, not knowing what this was about.

"Last spring," started Marlow, "someone compromised the third-floor offices with a break-in."

Rebecca, Anthony, and Pinkish sat in silence.

" We are concerned about your safety," he continued. "If you continue to work on the third floor, you need to be aware of your surroundings and report any suspicious activity. Notify Dean Gallagher or call me. I will give you my contact information before I leave. Dr. Bloom suggested Ms. Monahan not work in the office in the future, as he is very concerned."

Rebecca objected. "Surely I am not the target; I would like to continue to work, as usual. I'm not worried about the break-ins."

They all considered her comment, and Anthony offered a solution. "Pinkish and I will be on the floor while Ms. Monahan is present. Why not install a secure lock and allow her to continue in a locked office? I would be happy to escort her to her car, and we can keep an eye on her while she is working."

Dean Gallagher had to hide his smile. If he were thirty years younger, he too would offer to keep an eye on Ms. Monahan.

"I could escort her home if that is a concern; if she agrees."

Rebecca nodded, the blush on her fair complexion obvious. "That would be so nice of you, Anthony."

This interaction intrigued Mr. Marlow and Dean Gallagher. Pinkish knew the situation and was not surprised.

"So it's settled," concluded the dean. "Your group needs to be careful, and we would like to keep the incident confidential for now.

I suggest you proceed with your daily routine but be aware of your surroundings, and do not confront anyone on the floor after hours. Call us to report anything unusual."

Pinkish wanted to say something before the meeting ended. He was thinking about himself as well as Anthony and Rebecca. "Dr. Hall thinks we intrude while performing our duties on the third floor. It is not conducive to our livelihood."

"Dr. Hall will move his work to the second floor. He needs help from the staff since his assistant resigned. As of today, Dr. Bloom will be the only instructor on the third floor."

They were all relieved. Mr. Marlow handed his cards to the three students. "Call me with your concerns. I appreciate your cooperation."

Dean Gallagher asked Rebecca to stay when the meeting was over. He gave her an encouraging smile as the others left the office.

"Dr. Monahan, I spoke to the operative department, and they suggested you need more time doing operative procedures. Some of the credit from last semester will not be honored. They have added requirements to prepare you for private practice."

Rebecca felt a lump in her throat and tried to fight back the tears.

"This means you will not finish before graduation. You can walk with your class at graduation, and we will make every effort to provide you with the cases needed to complete the requirements. As you know, this semester the clinic is changing. One instructor will grade most procedures. I have placed you on the team with Dr. Curtis. He is easy to work with and teaches his students with the same practical approach that has guided him through years of a highly successful private practice."

Dean Gallagher saw the teardrops silently falling from Rebecca's stoic features. Her eyes were a bright blue-green, and she was staring at her hands, not daring to look at him for fear of losing her composure.

"I know this sounds disappointing," he said softly," but it will be a blessing in the long run. You will be better prepared for challenges after graduation, and I promise you will be learning from the very best."

Rebecca knew she had to suck it up and accept the advice of the instructors. She did not want to cry in the dean's office. The instructors would think she wasn't tough enough to finish dental school.

"Thank you for your help, Dean Gallagher. I am sure Dr. Sherman and Dr. Cavit know what is best. I look forward to learning from Dr. Curtis."

She excused herself from the dean's office. She tried to leave before anyone saw how upset she was, but as luck would have it, she passed Dr. Bloom in the hallway. He saw she had been crying and insisted she accompany him to an empty classroom so she could talk about it.

"I have never seen you so upset, Rebecca. What happened?"

"I'm behind in my requirements," she admitted in a shaky voice, "and I will remain after graduation to get my degree. I can attend the graduation ceremony with my class but will stay behind through May and June. I'm the first to admit I need more help with operative dentistry."

Dr. Bloom tried to reassure her. "You are not the first student who was late in fulfilling the requirements and not the first who finished after graduation."

Rebecca gave him a hopeful look. He knew a moment like this could change everything and tried to find the right words of encouragement.

"Please don't feel bad about yourself, Rebecca," he said softly. "Some students in your class are too confident, and I worry about them. A big ego can lead to carelessness, and believe me, dentistry can be the most humbling of professions. In dentistry, it is impossible to achieve perfection, and regardless of who you are, there will be failures because of all the factors beyond your control. But I am not worried about you. I know you will always do your best, and your heart will always be in the right place. Patients will sense how much you care about your work, and your skills will forever grow and improve. You will be successful as a dentist."

Rebecca was so choked up she could hardly speak. "Thank you, Dr. Bloom. I really needed to hear that."

Chapter 18

The gruesome reality of the head and neck anatomy lab was soon apparent to the students. Although the process was done respectfully, the sad truth was that the only parts left in the lab were the head and neck. The rest of the body had been removed. Worse yet, the specimens were sectioned at the midline so structures could be studied from the inside out. Some students had volunteered to perform the disturbing task of cutting the head and neck in half. Afterwards, Dr Hall stormed into the dean's office to make a formal complaint.

"The male cadaver is not a suitable candidate for study; he had a head injury."

This troubled Dean Gallagher. "As you are aware, Dr. Hall, the medical school screens the cadavers. The records show he died of heart failure. They are not supposed to accept donations with head or neck injuries."

"Well, when I lifted the drape, the head injury became immediately visible to me."

Dean Gallagher notified Mr. Marlow and asked him to check all records. The dean wanted to know Charlie's real name and the circumstances of the donation process. Charlie was missing when Anthony, Pinkish, Amy, Joe, Roy, and Ron attended their first head and neck anatomy lab. The group dispersed, and the students studied different cadavers. Most students counted the days until they could put this lab experience behind them. Having a cadaver to study seemed like an interesting project until expected to continue it for many months. They were growing weary of the course. When their studies were over, the school held a memorial service for the cadavers. Anthony did not attend.

***

With a heavy heart, Rebecca resumed clinic. January was cold and dreary, and Anna approached her with more disturbing news that first week. "Rebecca, I have something to tell you about one of your patients. I just saw Jake Murray for a restoration, and he told me his mother passed away over the holiday."

"My denture patient, Mrs. Murray? I just saw her a few weeks ago. What happened?"

" She had cancer but kept it to herself. She knew it was terminal. Jake told me the denture you inserted made her happy."

"She didn't tell me. I went over her medical history, and she never mentioned cancer or any treatment she was receiving. I feel awful."

"Jake said she refused treatment; it was Stage IV cancer, and a cure was unlikely. He said she had been in pain, but now she is at peace."

"Oh my God, he's a teenager, and he just lost his mom. And she was only in her forties."

Rebecca had to run to the ladies' room. She wondered if she would cry every time a patient died, certainly, it would always affect her. No wonder Mrs. Murray was requesting medication for pain; she was nearing the end of a terminal illness. Rebecca felt guilty for misjudging her patient and for being unable to help her. She could have referred her to the hospital for pain management.

The next shock came later that month when Rebecca saw Blake Cooper scheduled as an emergency. She headed toward the waiting area to see what happened. "Hello Blake. Do you have an emergency?"

When Blake smiled, Rebecca gasped in horror. His central incisor #9 had broken in half.

"Were you in an accident?"

"Sorry to bother you, Doc, but this happened in hockey practice. I was hoping you might be able to fix it."

Rebecca brought Blake to X-ray and then brought him to her station for a plan of treatment. Dr. Curtis examined Blake. "How should we proceed, Dr. Monahan?" he asked.

Rebecca saw only one reasonable option. "Because of the loss of tooth structure, I think Blake needs a crown."

"I agree," remarked Dr. Curtis. "You can start the preparation and fabricate a temporary crown."

She had no problem preparing the tooth. Enough tooth structure remained for a crown, and the fractured tooth showed no sign of nerve damage. Replacing a single tooth in the anterior was a cosmetic challenge; and when she considered how attractive Blake Cooper was, the task seemed overwhelming. She did not want #9 to be the flaw in his good looks. But then she had a brilliant idea. A talented young lab technician worked in the school's crown and bridge lab. Rebecca asked her to meet Blake and do a custom shade match. She thought another young woman might feel the same responsibility when meeting Blake.

"Ms. Anderson, I would like to request a custom shade match for tooth #9. The patient is a young man, and, to put it bluntly, is extremely good-looking. He has little specks of fluorosis on his adjacent teeth. I hope to achieve a result that, to the average eye, will be unrecognizable as a crown."

Of course, every patient deserves the best result, but Ms. Anderson's curiosity and admiration led to special attention. She took a custom shade match along with photos and notes. The fluorosis would be difficult to mimic, but Ms. Anderson was an artist. She also was an available female, and Rebecca thought she saw her slip her business card into Blake's shirt pocket.

***

The mundane routine continued for the students. For Rebecca, a bright spot was the publication of the dental materials newsletter. The first edition received rave reviews. The plan was to publish quarterly, and Rebecca would be a part of the next two editions.

That January, it snowed and snowed. The students trudged to school every day, but patients cancelled because of the weather. Rebecca was gaining confidence under the supervision of Dr. Curtis, but she did not complete her requirements as quickly as she had hoped. It was too cold to walk to school, so Rebecca would bring her little red Mustang to the student lot. She hoped it would continue to withstand the elements. The car was normally reliable, but on a particular Saturday in January, it wouldn't start. The air was painfully cold; you could not breathe the outside air without a face covering. Rebecca then noticed there were no cars on the road. She gave up her plan to drive the car and returned to her apartment to turn on the news report. She hoped to see basketball highlights, which were usually reported on Saturday morning. A weather alert appeared on the screen instead.

'This morning at 3 am there was a record windchill well below zero. Please stay indoors if at all possible. If you must go outside, limit your exposure to 5 minutes.'

Rebecca decided there was no way she would spend another winter here.

Chapter 19

The oral surgery department was separate from the main clinic, with its own instruments, sterilization area, and appointment protocol. The juniors and seniors were assigned to the oral surgery block for a two-day rotation, and they performed all surgeries scheduled for those days. Most of the time, the patients needed routine extractions, but the students also removed impacted wisdom teeth. The schedule was slow because of the weather, and by Friday afternoon most patients canceled because of a storm warning. Students were required to remain on call. With nothing on the schedule, Rebecca seized the opportunity and asked the oral surgery instructor if she could be the patient. Getting her wisdom teeth removed was on her to-do list, and as a student, she could get it done for free. Soon Rich, her oral surgery partner, was administering the lidocaine assisted by a junior student she did not know, Jeff Muller. She had two upper wisdom teeth, as the lower ones were congenitally missing. The procedure went well, and Rebecca was getting post-op instructions when they got word the school would close early because of the storm.

The dental school's lower level lacked windows; but opening the door for exterior viewing revealed white-out weather conditions. The

4pm freshman lecture was canceled. Anthony assumed he would not stay after school for his custodial duties.

"Is it advisable to walk in this?" asked Pinkish.

"Not really," Anthony replied. "We should look for a ride home. We'll talk to Jeff about our hours."

They walked to the front desk to find out where he was. The clinic was already closed. The receptionist looked up Jeff's assignment for the afternoon and pointed them to oral surgery.

"He's in oral surgery," said Anthony. "Let's see if he's still there or if he left for the day."

When they entered the area, they saw Rich, Jeff, and a red-haired surgery patient holding an ice pack.

"But you can't drive home," complained Rich. "You are in no condition to drive, and we gave you post-op Percocet."

"I don't want to leave my car in the snow," insisted Rebecca. "I'm afraid they might tow it when they plow."

Jeff looked at Anthony and Pinkish and realized they were wondering about work.

"They canceled after-school work," said Jeff. "We heard it's a blizzard."

"We looked outside," exclaimed Pinkish, "and we will not be going home if we do not leave soon."

Anthony had his wisdom teeth removed, and he remembered how uncomfortable he had been afterward. He wanted to help Rebecca and offered his services. "Pinkish and I can dig out your car and drive to our neighborhood. We both need a ride, and you will have your car for the weekend."

"That sounds good, Anthony." She didn't want to say much with all the gauze in her mouth.

"If you give me your keys, Pinkish and I will bring your car to the front entrance."

Rebecca grabbed her purse and handed over the keys. "It's parked in the usual spot, near Farmland Dairy."

"I know where you park," commented Anthony before he could stop himself. Both Jeff and Rich looked at him with surprised awareness. They wondered how he knew Rebecca and how he was familiar with her car. She was sitting in the patient waiting area when Anthony and Pinkish returned to pick her up. The picture window gave her a pretty view of the swirling snow outside, and she watched as they entered the dental school.

"Surely you weren't planning to walk in this!" she remarked.

"We were hoping to find a ride, so this works for all of us."

Pinkish was nervous about the blizzard and eager to get home. They dropped him off first. Then they parked by Rebecca's apartment and Anthony helped her in. Neither one had thought through what was going to happen next.

"Do you want me to come in and help you get settled?"

"Yes, please."

Rebecca was feeling miserable since the lidocaine was wearing off and the Percocet was upsetting her stomach. She went to her room to change into sweatpants and a T-shirt. Anthony went into the kitchen and found chicken broth. He heated it and brought it to her.

"Thanks, Anthony, I didn't think this one through. I thought it might be a good idea to remove my wisdom teeth; that way Rich and Jeff could get some credits."

"It's fine, Rebecca. It is the type of thing you want to put behind you."

"Anthony, the prescription pain medication is wearing off, but is making me sick. There is regular Tylenol in the medicine cabinet. Could you get it for me?"

"Sure thing. Do you want to sleep after you have soup?"

"I'm not tired, Anthony. Could you sit with me? I should continue ice packs so I don't get swollen."

He tried to get Rebecca's mind off her discomfort by telling stories about his cousins in New Jersey, and spoke of his parents and siblings. Anthony shared his story about his last-minute offer for dental school and how he met Chuck. The whole time she gazed at him as if he were the most fascinating guy on the planet. He appreciated her interest, but wasn't used to talking about himself.

Rebecca couldn't believe what a nice guy Anthony was. The sound of his voice had a soothing effect on her. He was so gentle when he helped her change her gauze or when he fluffed up her pillows. She knew that as a dentist he would have a wonderful chairside manner. Something was very intimate about the way he cared for her, and she had an overwhelming desire to touch him. She placed her hand on the tiny scar visible on his chin.

"Now that," he started, "has a story behind it. I played baseball from the time I was in first grade until my senior year in high school. I made varsity but didn't get to play during games since it always seemed there was someone more talented than me. But at the end of my senior year, the right fielder sprained his ankle, and I finally got some playing time. It was the bottom of the ninth, tie score. When I got up to bat, I knew it was nearing the end of my baseball career, so when I felt a solid hit, I had to go with it. As I rounded third base, I knew it would be a close call to get home. But I had never hit a home run and somehow realized this would be my only chance. The outfielder threw the ball high, so I dove in hands first and tried to knock the catcher off balance. I was safe. Everyone cheered; we had won the game. But then I heard my mom screaming, and it was because I had slit my chin open and there was blood everywhere. It was great! Not only had I scored the winning run, I got everyone's attention since I was bleeding. Every day when I shave, I remember the time I went for it and everything turned out."

He looked at Rebecca; she was smiling, but she looked tired. He thought he should leave.

She somehow read his thoughts and spoke up. "Anthony, there is a blizzard outside. I hope you won't think I'm forward, but I think you need to stay here tonight. There are pillows and an extra blanket in the closet. You'll find a new toothbrush in the medicine cabinet. The living room is comfortable; I have fallen asleep on the couch many times."

"I'm used to sleeping on a couch," he replied. "Are you sure you don't mind?"

"Don't be silly, you can't walk home in this, and it would be hard to dig out the car tonight."

"I remember when I had my wisdom teeth extracted, I couldn't do anything myself. Call me if you need anything during the night. Good night, Rebecca."

"Night, Anthony."

He had trouble sleeping even though the couch was comfortable. Thoughts of Rebecca in the next room consumed him. He felt a thrilling tension between them even though she was in no condition to entertain thoughts of intimacy. Every encounter with Rebecca made him more helpless to resist her. Finally, he fell into a deep sleep, but in the morning he awakened to the sound of someone plodding up the stairs. Bright sunshine streamed through the living room windows. When he heard a gentle knock on the door, he answered. Ellen was on the landing with a snow shovel. Her eyes widened in surprise when she saw him. He was half asleep, dressed in a t-shirt and boxers, and since he had been dreaming of Rebecca when awakened, aroused and too embarrassed to confront anyone. He cracked the door open to Ellen.

"I'm sorry; I thought Rebecca might need help to clear her steps."

"Rebecca is asleep. Give me a minute to get dressed. I'll come out and do the walkway for her."

"Sounds good," said Ellen. "I will start clearing near the street."

Ellen thought that Rebecca had finally succumbed to her feelings for Anthony. She was glad it finally happened. Ellen imagined a romantic night together during a blizzard. Rebecca would normally be awake at this hour.

Ellen's obvious assumption embarrassed Anthony. He was half asleep and half dressed when he answered the door. He had a warm coat and gloves but would have to shovel in his sneakers. But he wasn't concerned about his footwear; after that dream and the unexpected knock on the door, he was more focused on the need to cool off. He walked down to the sidewalk and took the snow shovel from Ellen.

"I'll take over now, Ellen, right?"

"Yes, and you're Anthony, the pirate."

"Shall I call you Raggedy Ann?"

There was an awkward moment when neither knew what to say. They both smiled.

"Rebecca might be up now; I'm sure she would like to see you. She had her wisdom teeth out yesterday."

"She did? Rebecca didn't mention it to me. I would have been happy to help her."

"It was a kind of surprise appointment. Maybe you should look in on her. She might need help this morning."

"Thanks, Anthony. I'll do that."

Ellen wondered what bizarre circumstances must have led to this situation. She entered the apartment and took off her boots and outerwear, and couldn't help but notice the bedding when she walked past the living room couch. She opened the bedroom door. Rebecca was awake and looked swollen.

"Is Anthony still here? I heard you talking."

"No, he's outside doing the steps for you. He's a handy guy. I didn't realize the oral surgery department provided 24-hour care and a sexy nurse."

"It's another crazy story, Ellen. Are you sure he can't hear us?"

Ellen looked out the window. "No, he's clearing by the street first. You have a few minutes to explain."

"As you know, it started snowing around noon, and most of the patients canceled. We were in oral surgery block, and I thought if I got my wisdom teeth removed, Rich and Jeff would get some credits. It was a rash decision, but seemed like a good idea. Then they wouldn't let me drive, and I didn't want to leave my car in the lot; I was afraid campus security would tow it. Anthony was looking for Jeff when he entered the oral surgery department, and he saw my condition and offered to drive my car here. I asked him to stay over because of the blizzard."

"This is another confusing story, Rebecca, but you seem to be bleeding again, and I think you should talk some other time."

Ellen got new gauze for Rebecca and helped her get up to use the bathroom. "Just answer one question; you didn't sleep with him, did you?"

"Of course not."

Rebecca looked in the bathroom mirror. She looked pretty bad. If Anthony still liked her after seeing her like this, he was a keeper. Rebecca walked to the kitchen and continued the conversation. "That doesn't mean I didn't think about it. Though I was in pain from the neck up, I was still attracted to him. It was torture having him up here."

"Rebecca, you have been suppressing your feelings for him for months. Why don't you invite him over for dinner, maybe next weekend? As a thank you for taking care of you. He seems like a sweet guy."

"It's not that easy, Ellen. It is not fair to start something that will have to end. Besides, he's a freshman, and I know what that's like; he has to keep his head in the books."

"Shouldn't you leave that up to him? It might be worse to deny the feelings he has for you."

"He hasn't exactly asked me out."

"Well, then you need to make the first move. He must be waiting for you."

"That would be a first for me, Ellen. I don't know how to make the first move."

"It seems to me you already have. That night in September when you kissed him on your landing."

Just then, the girls heard a light tapping at the door. Anthony stood there rosy-cheeked and snow-covered but smiling when Ellen answered the door. "I don't want to track snow into the apartment, so I'll leave the patient in your capable hands."

But Ellen insisted. "Come in and get warm. I'm making coffee, or tea if you prefer. Then, I can drive you home if you help me clear off my car."

"Deal."

Rebecca enjoyed having both friends in her apartment. Anthony and Ellen had conversations about the snow, and then they talked about the Halloween party. Anthony told Ellen about Chuck and how disappointed he was when he didn't meet her at the party. Ellen had noticed the tall, imposing guy dressed as Zorro on Halloween. Although he was wearing a mask, she remembered he had a sexy smile.

"Chuck and I live next door to the medical students who had the party."

"Well, my roommate and I have known Rebecca for years, and live in the upstairs apartment next door. We have to watch our houses after the whole intruder business."

"What intruder?"

Rebecca finally spoke up. "It's nothing, Anthony. Some guy tried to follow me into my apartment."

Anthony was shocked and alarmed. "We should talk seriously about carpooling when you're working late."

Anthony helped Ellen clear off her car, and she gave him a ride back. He tried to get more information about the guy at Rebecca's door, but there wasn't much to say. He was protective and worried about circumstances that seemed to endanger her. Anthony would have to insist on bringing Rebecca home when she worked for Dr. Bloom.

Chapter 20

Chuck was looking out the window when he saw Ellen drop Anthony off in front of the house. He wondered what was going on. He was the one interested in Ellen; what was Anthony doing with her? Anthony had been out all night. Should he confront him, or act as if he hadn't seen them? He was upset and couldn't keep his feelings to himself.

"So it seems you're pursuing two girls now, Tony. What happened to the redhead?"

"You've got it all wrong, Chuck. I spent the night at Rebecca's apartment. Ellen just gave me a ride because I helped her clear off her car."

"So you finally made your move with the hot redhead?"

"It's not what you think, Chuck. She had her wisdom teeth out yesterday. I drove her home in the blizzard and helped her out."

"A likely story."

"Sad, but true. I told Ellen that you were interested in meeting her. I don't know when or if that will happen; I can't be responsible for your love life; I have enough trouble with my own."

"My heart bleeds for you, Tony. Most of us have to bend over backward to get the right girl interested. But all you pretty boys have to do is smile and they're sold."

"You don't know what you're talking about!"

"Don't I? You haven't even dated that gorgeous redhead that drifts in and out of your life, and already you've spent the night with her."

"It wasn't like that, Chuck. She had her wisdom teeth out. What were we supposed to do?"

"I can think of several things."

"Shut up, Chuck. You're pushing this too far, and I'm on the edge of furious right now."

Chuck decided to back off. Talking to Anthony about his night with Rebecca was a sore spot. He was quite certain that nothing had happened. The silence was deafening. He gave his roommate a concerned look. "You could have called. For all I knew, you could have frozen to death on the way home."

"Thanks for your concern, Chuck."

Anthony thought the entire conversation had gotten ridiculous. He knew they were both too stubborn to apologize. "So, Chuck, you think I'm pretty?"

"Shut up, Tony."

***

The extreme weather continued for several weeks. The freshmen and sophomore students proceeded as usual, but the students in the clinic experienced a slowdown. Rebecca had plenty of time to study under the tutelage of Dr. Curtis, and she was gaining confidence. The bad news was she had fallen further behind in requirements, and the new goal was to finish by the summer break in July.

Blake Cooper's crown was a great success. Rebecca was more excited about it than Blake. He didn't realize how hard it was to get a perfect match on an upper central incisor, especially since the shade had to be customized. Ms. Anderson admired her work, and the result impressed Dr. Curtis.

Rebecca's social life revolved around her activities with Ellen or Anna and the time she spent commuting with Anthony. On the days she planned to work, Anthony used his car to pick her up in the morning, then drove her back to her apartment at night. She wanted to ask him in, but she didn't trust herself and resolved to keep things casual. As their friendship deepened, this became more difficult.

Rebecca was soaking in the tub one Friday night when the phone rang. She rushed to answer it, thinking it could be Anthony.

"Hello."

"Hi, I'd like to speak to Rebecca Monahan." The voice sounded familiar, but she didn't recognize it.

"Speaking."

"This is Casey Jones calling from KQ98."

"You're kidding. Who is this really?"

"Casey Jones from KQ98. I'm calling about your letter to the radio station, and I'm happy to inform you that we've chosen your playlist for next Friday at 10 pm."

"Oh, thank you. I sent that in months ago."

"Well, it's a great list, and we're happy you're a KQ98 listener. Stay tuned, and next Friday night we will play Rebecca Monahan's personal music hour."

"Thank you, Casey."

After she hung up the phone, she called her friends. She would like to have them over to listen to the broadcast. The month had been so dreary, and it would be a good excuse to have a party. Ellen and Donna said they would come over. Anna was a maybe. She asked Anthony and Pinkish since they loved listening to music. Anthony wanted to hear what Rebecca had chosen for the hour; he was certain they had similar tastes in music. She asked Anthony to invite Chuck, though she doubted he could come over on a Friday night.

***

Anthony left a note for Chuck about Rebecca's invitation, since they kept different hours and rarely saw each other. Finally, they spoke on the day of the party.

"Tony, don't you know this is the night of the concert?"

"What concert?"

"The concert. Karl Santos. I closed the jazz club because of it. All of my customers will be at the concert."

"I didn't know. I guess you can't come to Rebecca's tonight."

"Why don't you give me her number? I might join you for a beer after the concert."

"I'll let her know."

***

They were in a festive mood that evening. The party was an unusual mix of dental, medical, and law students. Ellen and Pinkish hit it off; their conversation was easy and entertaining. Pinkish kept quiet at most parties since English was a second language, but Ellen encouraged him, and their comments were hilarious. Anthony was happy to see Pinkish come out of his shell. Ellen was always amusing and a natural storyteller; in fact, Anthony thought Ellen was the funniest person he knew, except for Chuck. Both were effortlessly entertaining and usually the life of the party. He wondered if they could become an item. Rebecca's friends enjoyed the music hour and lingered at her apartment after the broadcast. When the phone rang, Rebecca had trouble hearing the person on the other end but knew it was Chuck.

"Hello, I'm in a phone booth, and it's hard to hear. Is Tony there? It's important."

"Anthony, it's Chuck. Says it's important."

"Hi Chuck."

Chuck was so excited he could hardly contain himself. "Do you have the key to the club?"

"Yes"

"Good. Open the door, set the place up, and bring the party. Karl Santos is going to play for us."

"What?"

"I told him I own the only jazz club in town, and he agreed to stop in. We are all so excited. I want the establishment open and ready for customers in about 30 minutes. I am bringing a crowd with me."

"Fantastic, I'll do what I can." Anthony looked at the group of friends who were sensing the excitement. "Can you all come to Chuck's place with me? It's a rare opportunity to hear a famous jazz artist, Carl Santos. He'll be there soon."

They reached for their coats and scrambled to open the place. Ellen was the only one who knew of Carl Santos, and she assured them this was a big deal. The famous artist played with the local musicians that night, and the sound was magic. Chuck was on cloud nine and took plenty of photos. They were all impressed with Carl Santos; his talent and the fact that he took the time to visit his fans. After he left, the evening took an even more amazing turn for Chuck. He met Ellen. The two of them had a detailed conversation with Pinkish about jazz, and it was quite funny. Chuck and Ellen were comical together; they seemed to play off each other. Chuck was full of information and impressed that Ellen had an appreciation for jazz. He didn't hesitate to ask her out. She was too nice to say no on his special night, and he was not ashamed to use this to his advantage. He had been thinking about her since Halloween. She was beautiful; he admired her warm brown eyes, silky dark hair, and friendly smile. Although she tried to hide this particular asset, she was full-figured, and Chuck found this extremely attractive. He felt like a cad thinking about it; he was such a guy and couldn't pretend he didn't notice. After meeting her, Chuck realized there was something beyond beauty that intrigued him — the comfortable banter, the joking around, the way they interacted when telling a story. He knew they had a special connection, but she didn't see it. He was determined, more than ever, to make her a part of his life.

Chapter 21

Anthony looked back on the last few months and couldn't believe how much his life had changed. Six months ago he didn't know the friends that were so important to him now. He could have socialized more, since his class had a reputation for partying, but he was content to remain on the sidelines and nurture a close friendship with Pinkish, Chuck, and now Rebecca. Anthony often stayed home with Ralphie and listened to music. He longed to date Rebecca, but it seemed like she was only interested in friendship, and he decided he would not jeopardize that. So when the freshman class planned a big party in March, he wondered if he could invite her. A class party like that could be seen as a friend date. The theme was prom, but it was not a dental school-sanctioned formal affair; just an excuse for a fun party. The girls were planning to resurrect their old prom dresses, and many of the guys rented those pastel ruffled shirt tuxedos that have since gone out of style. If Anthony went alone, it would be a night of drinking. If he brought Rebecca, he could dance, which was one of his hidden talents, especially if he had a beer or two to loosen up. Ron Zee scheduled his band for the event; they were driving to the party from Chicago. During the ride home one night, Anthony found the courage to ask.

"My class is having a party, and I wondered if you would like to go with me."

"Sounds like fun, Anthony. When is it?"

"The last Saturday in March. It's a prom, but just for fun, nothing too formal or serious. We will have a live band and dancing."

Rebecca couldn't help but smile. She wondered what kind of dancer Anthony was. "I'd love to go. Tell me what I should wear."

"I guess any dress. I will wear a suit but accessorize with the crazy tie Angela made for me in fourth-grade sewing class. It has daisies on it. The idea is to dress up but not take it seriously; the theme being a throwback to our high school prom. The party starts at 9:00 but with drinks and hors d'oeuvres only. Maybe we could go to dinner beforehand?"

Rebecca smiled. "It's a date."

Those three words sent his spirit soaring. He would finally have the chance to take her out. He had three weeks of labs and exams to get through, so he didn't have time to dwell on it. They were finally exiting a brutal winter, and after prom, Easter and spring break would follow.

***

They had nearly forgotten the third-floor concerns. Anthony, Pinkish, and Rebecca remained diligent but had not seen or heard anything unusual since meeting with Mr. Marlow. Rebecca worked extra hours and would soon launch the next dental materials newsletter, seeing more of Anthony as a result. One evening when they were heading to the car, she realized she had left a notebook at her desk.

When she returned to the third floor, a man was breaking the lock on the office door. She tried to retreat down the stairs and started screaming for Anthony as the man pushed past her. Pinkish and Anthony ran toward her scream.

Pinkish ran to the skywalk and identified the perpetrator as he drove off. Pinkish couldn't see the license plates but saw the man in the distance. They called Mr. Marlow, who drove to the school to interview them.

Pinkish described the man as middle-aged, with a medium height and build, and the car was a mid-sized white sedan. Rebecca collaborated with him on this description, but neither saw the man's face. Rebecca said she got a good look at his left hand.' *Not much to go on,'* thought Marlow.

When Anthony drove Rebecca home the night of the incident, she was upset. He walked her to her door. "Are you going to be all right?" he asked.

"I'll be fine, Anthony, but I am becoming unnerved. I always took my safety for granted at school and in this neighborhood, but I no longer feel secure. These incidents prove there is cause for concern. But once again, thank you."

"What for? I wasn't able to do anything."

"You were there when I needed you. That is enough."

She looked into his intense blue eyes; the hunger and fire were unmistakable. She knew he wanted her. It would be so simple to ask him in.

"Good night, Anthony."

"I'll see you tomorrow, Rebecca."

She left him as he stood on the landing, her sexual awareness heightened, and she was more than ready for him to pursue her. She imagined what would have happened if she had asked him in. They would be so desperate they wouldn't reach the bedroom. The attraction was powerful, but the timing was unfortunate. What was she to do? Love him, then leave him? It was becoming clear that it was exactly what she would do. It was only fair that she be honest with him before this went any further. She felt like she would burn in hell. If she had relations with Anthony, there would be no future, only now. Still, she couldn't help herself. She wanted to be with him more than ever.

She went to her dresser to look for her pills. She stopped taking them last summer when she knew her relationship with Kyle was ending. They had kept her safe from unwanted pregnancies. Starting them would be a premeditated decision. She would start them at her next cycle and would give herself to him if he wanted her.

***

Another meeting in Dean Gallagher's office was about to begin, and Dr. Bloom was present. "Dr. Bloom" started Marlow, "it looks like you are the target. Do you have any idea what this is about?"

"There is something in the works," he replied, "but the project is not being done at the school."

"Have there been any break-ins at your house?"

"No, but the information is not there either. Once we secure the patent, I will be at liberty to talk. I doubt this is about my research, but I am beginning to wonder."

"Well, thank God no one was hurt," sighed the dean.

***

Dr. Bloom knocked on the office door as Rebecca was doing the final edit of the newsletter. She had a black coffee from the cafeteria; it was awful. "I have to stop drinking this," said Rebecca. "It's staining my teeth."

"I may be able to help you," replied Dr. Bloom." I am working on take-home bleaching products for patients. Follow my instructions, and the stains will dissipate. It's safe; I tried it on myself."

Even though he was older, Dr. Bloom had an attractive, clean-looking smile.

" Also, put a little milk or cream in the coffee. It will cause less staining."

Dr. Bloom gave her two bottles of liquid and instructions for use. "Have a colleague take upper and lower alginate impressions. Pour the models and trim the stone so there is a thin base and a hole in the middle for vacuum forming. Sam from the denture lab will show you how to vacuum form and trim the bleach trays. Before application, mix equal amounts of each liquid. This activates the bleach. Pour a small amount into your custom trays and wear them for an hour every night for about a week. If you experience sensitivity or are unhappy with the result, I can help with further instructions."

"Thank you, Dr. Bloom. I would love to bleach and quit coffee altogether."

Chapter 22

The night before prom, Anthony drove to the venue to help with preparations. The class had rented a big barn with a dance floor. It was popular for weddings and other occasions, but since there was no heat, it was rarely rented this early in the year. They would make do with space heaters since the drinking and dancing would keep them warm. A long bar ran along the back of the barn, and a small stage stood above the dance floor, used for bands or sometimes a caller for square dancing. The venue was the perfect place for a big event. As they prepared for the party, they experienced excitement that was contagious. Anthony brought his boom box, and the atmosphere was festive. He didn't know how to cook or make hors d'oeuvres, but Roy did and gave him instructions. Anthony had only one beer since he had to cut fresh vegetables with a scary-looking knife. He was proud of his vegetable platters when they were done and thought he might like to learn how to cook someday. It was fun preparing for the party; it was the beginning of the celebration to end a lengthy and dreary winter.

***

Rebecca wore her little black dress for their night out. The idea was to dress for fun, so she accessorized with costume jewelry, a shell necklace from the New Jersey shore, and shell earrings. She thought Anthony might enjoy the reference to the sea. She had almost forgotten about them; she hadn't worn them since high school and was surprised to find them in her jewelry box. Rebecca looked glamorous in her black dress and heels. Anthony had not seen her dressed up since that first night at the jazz club, and she wanted to look attractive for him.

When Anthony arrived at her apartment, he had a corsage for her. He was stunned when he saw Rebecca. She was made up for a night out and looked like a model. He had never dated a woman who looked so captivating and sophisticated, and he felt nervous. As soon as he took her hand, he relaxed; being on a date didn't change things.

"Do you like Mexican food?" he asked.

"I love it; the spicier, the better."

"That somehow doesn't surprise me."

"What are you trying to imply?"

"Only that I think you're hot in all possible ways. I would expect you to order extra spice. And by the way, I like the mermaid vibe. Is the jewelry from the Jersey Shore?"

"It is. I'm still trying to lure you to the sea."

He took her hand and gazed at her quite seriously. "You don't have to try very hard. I'm yours."

The restaurant had a festive atmosphere as the tables and chairs were bright with bold Mexican designs; candles were everywhere. Dinner was casual and very relaxed. They each ordered a frozen margarita and requested extra spice in the salsa. Anthony and Rebecca enjoyed the dinner date so much that they lost track of the time.

They were late getting to the party, but Pinkish saved seats at their table. Roy, Joe, and Amy brought dates. Rebecca sat between Pinkish and Anthony, and the two guys shared her during the party. Pinkish was interesting as a dancer since he brought Bollywood moves to the dance floor, and Rebecca had fun trying to follow him. Anthony was relaxed and uninhibited as a dancer, and in sync with the music. Even though it was a rock band, Rebecca suspected he had ballroom in his background. Ron Zee performed all night with his band. Rebecca thought there was nothing like live music at a party, and she had a fabulous time. The band featured guest vocalists from the class, which made it especially fun. It took courage for these amateurs to join the band and sing, and it was toward the end of the first set when Ron stopped by the table.

"Tony, you're up."

Anthony looked around at his friends. "I apologize to you and George Harrison for what I'm about to do."

Rebecca sensed what was about to happen, and she was nervous for him. She already knew he had a marvelous voice, but she wasn't sure if he ever sang in public. There was a hush in the room when Ron played the iconic guitar intro to George Harrison's '*What Is Life?*'

Anthony started hesitantly, but then the girls in his class started screaming and pretending to swoon. That was all the encouragement he needed. He sang to Rebecca, and the lyrics were so romantic she wondered if he meant to say the words to her. The transformation of the quiet Anthony Roselli surprised the partygoers. He showed talent both on stage and on the dance floor; he appeared with a gorgeous date, and he shed his reserved, orderly personality for a far more animated one. Rebecca wasn't surprised. Anthony was waiting to reveal himself as the man he wanted to be; all he needed was more confidence.

Rebecca experienced an awkward moment with Amy in the ladies' room. Amy cornered her and started asking prying questions in a not-so-friendly way.

"So how do you know Tony?"

"We work together on the third floor of the dental school."

"What do you do?"

"I work for Dr. Bloom." She didn't want Amy to know she was a senior or a student. Amy could ask Anthony if she wanted, and Rebecca did not offer more information.

"You know, he's from my hometown," added Amy. "We used to date."

Rebecca heard the jealousy in Amy's voice. She thought about Amy crying in his arms in the freshman lab. There must be unresolved feelings between them. But Amy had brought a date, and she shouldn't be interested in Rebecca's date. Normally, Rebecca would not confront an ex-girlfriend, but she wasn't about to let Amy ruin an otherwise flawless evening. She left before Amy could ask anything else, but not before adding, "Anthony is a fun date. I'm glad he brought me."

The evening was over too quickly. Anthony stayed to help with the cleanup, and the organizers encouraged everyone to take a few beers with them. There was so much left over. He carried bottles of Michelob to the car, and they drove to a nearby park to talk and to have a beer. " Isn't this what you're supposed to do after prom? Park someplace and drink beer?"

"Is that what you did at your prom, Anthony?"

"I didn't go to prom. This is my first."

"Well, you didn't miss much. I wish I had stayed home. It's a shame they waste prom on high school students."

Anthony gave her a serious look. He was debating whether he should talk about his past. After all these years, it still hurt a little.

"I think you want to tell me why you didn't go to prom," she said in a soft, comforting whisper.

"OK, but I don't want you to feel sorry for me. It was a long time ago."

She waited as they sipped their beer.

"So, I was supposed to go to my prom, but my date dumped me last minute and went with someone else. The crazy thing is she encouraged me until I asked her; she was aware of my infatuation, and it was easy for her to get an invitation from me. I soon realized she was probably more interested in my brother Tommy than in me. My brother barely noticed her and would not have considered dating a high school girl, though I'm sure she was used to going out with older guys. Before the prom, Tommy warned me about her coming on to him, and I knew he was trying to protect me. Still, I wanted to go and hoped that a night of fun and dancing would bring her closer to me. The whole thing was a disaster. I had the tuxedo and even had a corsage when she told me she had made other plans. It hurt, but I didn't want my parents to know or feel sorry for me, so I drove to my brother's college dorm on prom night. To this day, my parents still don't know I missed prom."

"Anthony, I'm sorry."

"I thought you weren't going to feel sorry for me." He smiled. She stroked his hair and moved closer. He thought the sympathy was worth the humiliation he had just endured.

"She must have been crazy because if I were going to choose anyone to be my prom date, it would be you."

And then she moved closer still. She gave him a sultry look. "Since this is prom night and we're sitting here drinking beer in the dark, aren't we supposed to make out?"

In a matter of seconds, she was in his arms. They hadn't kissed since the Halloween party, and the months of longing only intensified the attraction. They were both burning with desire, but unsure how this prom evening should end. Fate intervened and decided for them.

After a few minutes, Anthony cracked open the steamy car windows. He heard voices that seemed to be approaching the car. "These damn teenagers shouldn't be out this late," he said jokingly.

Then there was a tapping on the window and a foreign voice. "So sorry, are you two making up?"

The intruders were Pinkish and Don Hsu. They were giggling like little girls. They were in the park smoking something.

"Do you need a ride home?" asked Anthony.

"Sorry, but yes, we are lost."

"Get in the back seat, guys."

The broken mood made Rebecca think it was for the best. She felt she should talk to Anthony before things went any further, and she didn't want to end the prom night with a discussion of her leaving. She asked to be driven home first, and Anthony complied. The evening had been a dream come true for him, but in his dream, it wouldn't have ended at her doorstep.

She kissed him as they lingered on the landing. "I had a wonderful time tonight, Anthony. It was like magic. This is the only prom I'll remember."

"Me too," he said with a smile.

Chapter 23

Anthony dropped off Pinkish and Don at the apartment Pinkish rented. They were high and inebriated, and Anthony thought it best if they stayed together. When Anthony drove home, Chuck had just finished work and was waiting for him.

"How was prom?"

"Outstanding!"

"Was Rebecca a fun date?"

"She was. We had an epic date; she was even comfortable talking to my goofball friends. You should have seen her dancing Bollywood with Pinkish."

"How about you? Did you sing?"

" I pulled it off, but only because of the margarita and the beer preceding the performance. Truthfully, it was fun."

"Good. Maybe you could learn some jazz numbers."

Anthony gave him a doubtful look. "I'm not ready to quit my day job, Chuck."

Chuck grinned. He thought with time he could wear him down.

"Easter is next Sunday. We could invite Ellen and Rebecca over for Easter dinner."

"We don't know how to cook Chuck."

"How hard could it be? I remember my grandmother baking ham and potatoes in the oven. I could do that. You chopped vegetables on Friday, and you could do that too. I'm sure the girls would help once they got here."

"I don't know when Rebecca is in town during the break, but I will ask."

"So when is your next date?"

"I don't know."

"What! Tony, you must strike when the iron is hot. She might think you don't want another date."

"I'm sure she knows."

"You can't take anything for granted. It was a mistake not to set up the next date. But you can redeem yourself. You could send flowers in the morning."

"Do you think I should?"

"Absolutely. I honestly don't know how you have captured the interest of such a beautiful creature. Sometimes I think you're clueless, Tony."

"Thanks for the vote of confidence, Chuck."

Anthony thought Chuck was right. Sending flowers was an idea. It would give him an opening to ask about Easter, though he could see the meal as being a disaster.

Rebecca called the next day when she received the flowers, but Anthony was at the library. Chuck answered the phone and took the initiative to ask about Easter.

"I am staying in town for the break, Chuck. Are you guys going to cook?"

"Yes, Tony and I have already discussed what we want to prepare. I have to work at night, so we'll have dinner in the afternoon."

"Sounds like fun. Can I bring anything?"

"Just yourself."

***

The freshman had exams that week, and the hardest one was neuroanatomy. Dr. Hall gave confusing lectures, and the textbook covered too much depth for the short time they had to learn the material. Anthony feared he was teetering on the brink of failure, just like first semester. Head and neck anatomy was in its final days. Dentists had to be familiar with the nerves and musculature surrounding the oral cavity, but Anthony was ready to finish the study. After studying cadavers all year, he doubted he would have the stomach to do any dissections in the future.

Rebecca knew he was exhausted, and she wanted to help him. She asked how he was holding up.

"Anthony, are you prepared for the exam week?"

"Not really, I wish I had better notes."

"Stop in a minute. I might be able to help."

Anthony was sitting at the kitchen table when she brought out her notes from freshman year. "A classmate of mine is a very organized student. His notes saved me freshman year, especially in neuroanatomy. Take these notes and read them over. The material will make more sense when you see how he organized his notes."

"Thanks, Rebecca. Why are you being so nice to me?"

"Because you let me." She gave him a kiss that energized him. He could be with her, and did not have to hide that he was vulnerable. Anthony often wished he could be more mature and stronger, and wondered if his youth and inexperience troubled her.

***

Rebecca and Ellen wore pretty flower-print dresses for Easter. The guys dressed for comfort. The ham and potatoes were in the oven as they enjoyed a bottle of wine. Rebecca and Anthony prepared the salad; Chuck had done all the shopping. When Anthony gathered the ingredients, he looked curiously at the lettuce. "Rebecca, there's something wrong with this lettuce."

Rebecca looked over. "It's cabbage."

"What?"

"Your lettuce is cabbage."

"Can we use it in a salad?"

Rebecca thought it hilarious that neither Chuck nor Anthony noticed this mistake. She thought she could make a save. "Do you have a cheese grater, mayonnaise, and Italian dressing?"

"Yes."

"Carrots?"

"Yes."

" I can make coleslaw with the cabbage."

He was relieved and hoped this was the only dinner setback. When Ellen and Chuck took Ralphie for a walk, Rebecca saw the opportunity to have a heart-to-heart talk with Anthony. She dreaded the discussion and hated the reality, but the talk was imminent. She looked at him, with longing and hope in her eyes.

"I wonder where this is going, Anthony. What do you think of me? About us?"

"God, Rebecca, where do I start? You're beautiful inside and out. I think about you all the time. I want to spend more time with you and wish our circumstances were different."

"You know I'm leaving. I will stay longer to finish my requirements but plan to move at the end of June." They looked at one another, saddened by their reality. She continued. "I wonder if we should see each other under the circumstances. It will be hard if we become attached."

"I'm already attached," he whispered. He tried to hide the pained expression on his face but knew the decision was hers. "What do you want, Rebecca?"

She was silent for a long time, then she answered him.

"I want time to get to know each other and see where it leads us. I wish we were in the same dental school class and had another three years to work together and help each other through. Of course, what I want is impossible, and I wonder how much it will hurt when I move back to New Jersey."

Anthony took her hand. He was certain of what he wanted to do. "I'm tired of living in the future. I gave up so much in undergraduate because I was studying and trying to get into dental school. I missed concerts and opportunities to travel, and I felt like I sacrificed my college years for a dream that almost didn't happen. Last summer, when I thought I wouldn't go to dental school, I wondered what I had done, and regretted not living the life I wanted as an undergraduate. Then, a decision by another student and a 5-minute phone call abruptly changed my life again. I can't live in the future any longer. I don't want to think about what happens next. I want to be with you, even if it's only for a short time. I'll take whatever we can have right now."

"I feel the same way, Anthony."

They felt the sad reality of their situation and held on to each other. But then Anthony's mood brightened when he thought about the spring break and the upcoming week. "We'll be in town this week.

Let's have some fun. On Tuesday, the weather is supposed to be in the 70s. Let's plan a day trip."

"I'd like that, Anthony."

Chuck and Ellen returned from their walk. Chuck started baking the cake when he took the ham out. He didn't think of preparing it ahead of time. He also burned himself when handling the ham. "Damn it."

"Are you hurt?" asked Anthony.

"I'm fine," he rumbled.

But then Ellen appeared, took his hand, and started running it under cold water. Anthony and Rebecca noticed his wink as Ellen took care of his injury. They allowed Chuck to enjoy the sympathy and left him alone with Ellen. They set the table and carved the ham.

"So what will we do on Tuesday?" she asked.

" I don't know if I can set it up, but I'd like to take you sailing."

Chapter 24

When Anthony picked Rebecca up on Tuesday morning, the weather was mild. Unsure of how she should dress, she wore shorts and a T-shirt and brought a change of clothes. She wondered if she would get wet on the sailboat. Even though she had the fair complexion of a redhead, she loved the sun and, if careful, could get a tan. Anthony brought a picnic lunch; she packed apples and grapes from her refrigerator. They were both eager and smiling; for Rebecca, it was a new adventure, and for Anthony, a chance to revisit his love of sailing. His old Cadillac was roomy and comfortable for the drive, and Rebecca settled into the passenger side and sipped the coffee to go.

"How did you know I needed this?"

"I took the chance you wouldn't have time to brew a cup this morning."

"Mm, it has cream and sugar. Delicious."

"I heard you have given up drinking it black."

" I have."

"I called Uncle Mark on Monday, and he will leave the boat on the trailer near the launch. The marina lounge will be open. Uncle Mark was happy to have us use the boat; he said it had remained dormant all last year."

"When was the last time you sailed?"

"It's been four years, and I truly miss it. I intended to use the boat more often, but didn't make an effort to drive to the lake. As a teenager, I spent two summers at the lake, worked at the marina, and stayed with Uncle Mark and Aunt Sophie. It was a highlight of my years in high school; by then their five boys were adults and on their own, and they always teased I was their sixth child."

"It sounds like you have cool relatives, Anthony."

"They're so nice, and I miss spending time with Uncle Mark. We were always close."

He continued in describing the boat. "The sailboat is a catamaran with a large mast, brightly colored sails, and a trampoline; since there is no bin for our gear on the boat, we will use a bungee cord to hold our belongings in place. The boat has been in storage, so we will set it up, raise the mast, attach the sails, and secure the rigging. It will take about an hour for the two of us to get it ready."

Rebecca was determined to be a good crew. She didn't know what she would have to do, but she was athletic and thought she could be helpful. The car ride took about 90 minutes; it was a scenic drive, and Anthony had a great selection of music on cassettes. Their conversation was lively. They stopped at a local Hinky Dinky and picked up a six-pack for Uncle Mark, and Rebecca bought spring flowers for Aunt Sophie.

And then they arrived. The morning was still, and the lake was calm, the breeze gentle. The lake had many coves. A few men fished in rowboats, but Anthony and Rebecca manned the only sailboat on the lake. After an hour, the boat was set up and in the water. It was a strenuous task, but they were a productive team, and Rebecca knew he couldn't have accomplished it without her. She couldn't believe it when Anthony asked her to hold the boat while he parked the trailer, and as she steadied it she admired the huge mainsail. Rebecca managed the smaller sail on the front of the boat, the jib. She learned to respond to Anthony's commands, like 'sheet in' or 'prepare to tack'. He was a patient instructor and explained different parts of the boat, upwind and downwind, and even how to predict the behavior of the wind by observing the telltales on the sail and watching the ripples in the water. Her role on the jib was instrumental in handling the vessel.

She fell in love with sailing. She was also falling for the captain of the ship. He was a dashing figure, and she could see the pirate, swashbuckling, unafraid and ready for adventure. Rebecca admired her handsome date; his white-collared shirt showed off a healthy tan, and he was well-rested and beaming. The sun was shining on them, and the conditions were perfect; when the wind picked up in the afternoon, they were ready. It was smooth sailing even in the gusty and changing winds.

Anthony suggested they break for lunch as they approached a scenic beach on an island. They loosened the sails and pulled the boat onto the sand. He led them to a grassy area up a hill with a panoramic view of the lake. The area was tree-lined and sheltered from the wind, and the sun's warmth made it feel like a summer day. Anthony brought a sheet, two towels, and a small cooler onto the grassy overlook. Rebecca never knew that ham, cheese, and tomato sandwiches could taste so good. They fed each other grapes, and Anthony brought the little chocolate doughnuts he knew Rebecca liked.

As they lay in the sun, Rebecca realized the day was perfect. She closed her eyes and savored what the weather was offering her. The afternoon sun was deliciously warm, but a gentle breeze caressed them. The sounds of spring flooded their senses; the birds singing, the tiny new leaves fluttering in the wind, and the calming sound of the waves on the shore left her refreshed and energized.

Rebecca was not able to relax. The sexual tension that crackled between her and Anthony was amplified by the sensory overload of the day and the fact that they were alone on a secluded island. She looked over at him while he had his eyes closed. He was a beautiful man, tall and lean with powerful arms and shoulders, and his presence overwhelmed her senses.

Anthony kept his eyes closed and tried to compose himself. Lying on the grassy overlook with Rebecca was overwhelming. His usual self-control and discipline had somehow abandoned him. Their fingertips touched lightly, but the thrilling tension was surging because she was beside him and they were alone. He hoped she would not notice his arousal.

She noticed. Rebecca never imagined this day trip would take a sexual turn, but now that they were in this sheltered, secluded oasis, she wasn't so sure. She leaned into Anthony and started caressing his neck. She melted into him as he wrapped his arms around her, and when he faced her, she saw hunger and fire in his eyes. Still, he kept his composure, and though his gentle kisses were passionate, he avoided any move that could make her feel pressured. His hands were gentle as he stroked her hair, her face, her shoulders, her arms. Yet she yearned to have him touch her more intimately. Rebecca knew that she would have to be the seductress, and subtly would not work. She hesitated, then continued because she was so sure he wanted her.

He watched her remove her shorts. She reached for him and unsnapped his. She touched him, and he felt unimaginable heat and desire.

"My God, Rebecca."

"Do you still want to be lured, Captain Roselli?"

He lost his breath for a moment. "Yes," he whispered, "I've been dreaming of it. You have no idea how much I want to."

She felt his hand tremble as he touched her face and her hair. She cupped her hand over his. "I'm a little nervous, Anthony."

As he gazed into her eyes, he never imagined a woman would ever look at him with such need, such want, so open and willing. He could not believe this red-haired goddess in front of him had chosen him. And suddenly, the act was beyond thought, beyond doubt. He was in love with her, and it all became simple.

"Are you sure?" he asked.

"I'm sure."

He removed his shorts and focused on those captivating aquamarine eyes; he held her tight, then placed her on top of him. She was smiling and couldn't stop kissing him. They were in awe of the gift they were about to give each other, and anxious for the journey they were about to take. In a move that seemed as natural as breathing, he became a part of her. Their lovemaking started slowly but became exceedingly passionate and urgent; they both held back because they didn't want it to end, and when the tension hit a heightened crescendo, he stilled her because he knew he could not last much longer. Her hair was cascading around him, and he was deep inside her as he tried to tell her something. "Rebecca ... "

Her response to the sound of his voice was surprising and overwhelming. He awakened something in her that she never knew existed. She clung to him and wanted to scream, but what came out was barely a whisper ... "Anthony,"

She abandoned herself to him with unrestrained pleasure, and he instinctively navigated her thrilling ride as they plummeted into a sea of passion. Swept into the crashing waves and the tumultuous seas, the voyage completed them and was far more fulfilling and satisfying than they ever imagined.

After their wild passage through a sea of emotion and his passionate release, he harbored gently as she embraced him. He stroked her hair, and she basked in his warmth and his love. As she clung to him, she marveled at his strength and his gentleness, and the faint scent of Old Spice made her believe she had just made love to a pirate. Rebecca waited for him to say something, but he remained silent and held onto her as though he was reluctant to let her go. She finally realized how exposed they were, and even though the location was remote, they had no guarantee of privacy. She wanted to hold on indefinitely, but knew they should get dressed. Finally, she lifted her head and gave him a curious look.

"Are you okay?" was the ridiculous question that came out of her mouth.

He gave her a rakish grin. "I'm more than okay, Rebecca; how about you?"

"I'm more than okay too, Anthony."

Then she left him, put herself together, and gathered their belongings. He held out his hand, and they walked in silence down the slope to the boat. The sail back to the marina was enchanting. The lake was calm, but a gentle breeze carried them along. It was the golden hour, and the lake sparkled like diamonds. But Anthony saw the genuine treasure on the boat with him. Highlights in her hair made her look like an angel, and the sun kissed her complexion in a most attractive way. He tried to sear this vision into his memory, for he realized this was a rare moment, one he would never forget.

When they reached the marina, Uncle Mark was waiting for them. He helped them drag the boat onto the beach in a spot where it would remain for the summer. They lowered the sails and secured the rigging.

"Uncle Mark, this is Rebecca."

"Hello Rebecca," he said as he gave her a handshake and a warm smile. "How do you like sailing?"

"I loved sailing; it was the best day ever."

"She was quite a crewman," added Anthony. "Quick to learn and possessing good instincts."

Uncle Mark looked at Rebecca's red hair and fair complexion. "Are you at all Irish or Scottish?"

"I'm both," replied Rebecca.

"Well, there you go; it's in the blood. There were many famous Scottish and Irish sailors. John Paul Jones was Scottish."

Rebecca gave him a happy smile. Then they noticed a woman waving from a nearby house.

"That's Sophie," said Uncle Mark. "She wants to meet you. Why don't you go over, Rebecca; she has some snacks for your ride home."

"Oh, the flowers!" Rebecca picked up the vase and spring flowers she had left by the dock. She walked over to meet Aunt Sophie.

Uncle Mark gave Anthony an approving look. "She's lovely," he said. Anthony smiled. But then Uncle Mark cleared his throat and took on a more serious tone. "Be careful, Anthony."

"Yes, sir."

Uncle Mark suspected the young couple had been intimate while on the island. He noticed the tall sailboat beached for most of the afternoon and that Anthony was beaming when they reached the marina. It was easy to figure out what had happened, and Anthony was never one who could hide his feelings. Uncle Mark had been young and was well aware of the allure of a secluded beach. Uncle Mark knew of their lovemaking, but Anthony was sure his uncle would keep it to himself.

Rebecca stayed for a few minutes to visit with Aunt Sophie. The two women were drawn to each other and easily engaged in conversation. They both had something in common; they both loved Anthony. It was dark as Anthony and Rebecca headed for the car, and they chose a cassette titled 'Love Songs' for the ride home. They drove home in comfortable silence as they tried to comprehend the enormity of the intimacy; the day was beyond words, and reality had been better than fantasy. She recognized a pattern when she listened to his cassette. Anthony had chosen songs with the most romantic lyrics. '*Annie's Song'* by John Denver, *'Make it with You'* by Bread, *'We May Never Pass This Way' Again'* by Seals and Crofts, *'Longer'* by Dan Fogelberg; and *'You're the Inspiration'* by Chicago. Only a romantic man would put these songs together. Rebecca wondered if he knew the day would be special.

When they arrived at Rebecca's apartment, he wasn't sure what to say or do. He had already kissed her hundreds of times that day, and a kiss didn't seem like enough. So when they reached the door, he took her hand. "Thank you, Rebecca. Today I enjoyed the two things I love most in life: sailing and being with you. I wish I had words to describe my feelings, but I don't think there are words. The day was epic." He kissed her hand, then turned it over and kissed her wrist, and the kiss touched her pulse and radiated straight to her heart. She wanted him all over again.

"Until next time," he said, and with a grateful smile he watched her open her door, not realizing that once again he had left her breathless.

Chapter 25

When Anthony walked into his kitchen, Chuck and Ralphie were waiting for him. He wasn't hungry, but thought he should eat something more substantial than the snacks he had on the ride home. Chuck took a long look at Anthony.

"So you two finally did it," he said as a matter of fact.

Anthony turned red from the neck up. *What the heck,* he thought. *Am I so easy to read? Do I have a scarlet letter on my chest?*

"My personal affairs are none of your concern," he said coldly.

Chuck let it go. He didn't want to put a damper on Anthony's day and suspected it might have been a first for Anthony. Chuck was happy that Anthony had experienced sex with someone amazing like Rebecca. Then Anthony felt bad about his sharp response, though Chuck could have kept his thoughts to himself or at least not have been so blunt.

"We had an epic day sailing. How are things with you and Ellen?"

"I'm working my way into her heart. She's resistant, but I think she likes me. Do you think I'm too anxious?"

"Yes, but that's who you are, Chuck. Don't change."

They both grinned, realizing how lucky they were to have such outstanding girlfriends. Chuck needed another guy to talk to. As far as Anthony could tell, his other friends just wanted to talk about jazz.

***

The next morning, Rebecca found it difficult to function. Her mind was a million miles away as she sat at her kitchen table. Mr. Grilli blasted Debby Boone's *You Light Up My Life.* Debby knew what it was like to be head over heels in love. Rebecca barely heard the knock on the door. Ellen. Rebecca wondered how her friend always sensed she needed to talk.

"Good morning. What's going on? I knocked, and you didn't hear me."

"Sorry, Ellen. Mr. Grilli is blasting his music."

"How was your sailing date?"

"I don't know where to start. Sailing was amazing, the date was amazing, and I'm falling for Anthony."

"That sounds serious, Rebecca. Did anything special happen?"

Rebecca blushed, and then Ellen thought she knew what had happened. "Did he make love to you yesterday?"

Rebecca sighed. "He did. I never knew it could be like that, or that I could feel the way I do."

"I understand," said Ellen.

"No, I'm sure you don't. I never knew I could lose myself like that. Anthony took me someplace unimaginable, and I honestly didn't know it could be like that. Now I understand why women will change their plans for a chance to be alone with their boyfriends."

Ellen gave her a knowing look. Then she put on her physician's hat. "You need to answer these three questions: Do you trust him? Does he make you feel safe? Does he take your breath away?"

"Yes, to all three questions."

"Has anyone else been a yes to those questions? An intimate relationship between a man and a woman is complex; besides being physical, it's hormonal and emotional, and so much of the sex occurs in your mind."

"You are so right, Ellen. I never thought of it that way."

"Anthony is right for you, and you could abandon yourself to him. That is why you reached your full potential sexually."

"You are so smart, Ellen. You should be a physician."

Both girls smiled.

"Why don't you call Anthony and invite him over? He has been spending too much time in the library; he wants to give Chuck space when I visit. But it is Anthony's spring break, and he should not be in the library all week."

Rebecca was happy to have an excuse to invite Anthony over. "I'll call him right now. He can stay with me the entire week if he wants."

***

Anthony said he would be over after he took Ralphie for a walk. He didn't know what to expect, or if seeing Rebecca would feel awkward. He experienced a sense of euphoria after their intimacy on the beach, but Uncle Mark's warning troubled him. The turn of events was unexpected, and neither of them anticipated what transpired between them during a sunny day of sailing. As far as he knew, no precautions had been taken; he should have been careful with her. He knocked on her door and peered through her window. The kitchen was bright with the morning sun, and Rebecca looked beautiful, vivid, enchanting, and sun-kissed. He felt a fierce, powerful attraction for her — the anticipation of spending time alone in the apartment set fire to his blood. But first, they had something to discuss. When she let him in, he headed for the kitchen table.

"Coffee?" she asked.

"Yes, please."

She gave him a curious look as she imagined the morning would be more physical than verbal. But he was struggling to talk about something. She hoped he didn't think that yesterday was a mistake.

"I'm sorry, Rebecca. I should have been careful with you; I'm afraid I'm not a very good Boy Scout."

She looked at him with curiosity; she didn't know what he was talking about.

"I wasn't prepared, and I didn't expect to ... I would never want to do anything to hurt you."

Then Rebecca caught his drift. "Well, Anthony," she started, "I thought being prepared was the Girl Scout motto. And although I was not a good Girl Scout, I am prepared since I've been dreaming about us for quite a while."

Anthony was relieved. "You have?"

They both smiled at each other.

"How long have you been thinking about being with me?" he asked.

"Well ... I had to leave you on the porch Halloween night because I was thinking about it then."

"You were?" Anthony could not believe what he was hearing. All that talk about Rebecca and her bad luck with men and how he needed to be careful with her was false.

"It wasn't until we became friends I believed it would happen. When did you think you wanted me?"

"On the day I saw you in the third-floor office last August. I was smitten, never dreaming I would be in your apartment."

She took his hand and led him to her bedroom. "We've wasted too much time, Anthony." She wanted him; this time there was no hesitation. She looked so soft and lovely as she waited for him to join her on the bed, and he couldn't believe how beautiful she was. He kissed her, and soon she was begging for him. They were fearless, adventurous, and wonderfully compatible, and the privacy of Rebecca's apartment gave them complete freedom. For once, she was grateful for Mr. Grilli's loud music.

The week became a staycation for Rebecca and Anthony. They went hiking and saw the movie Ellen had talked about, *'Foul Play'*, with Chevy Chase and Goldie Hawn. They partied at the jazz club on Thursday night and met Ellen there. After a few drinks, the girls convinced him to sing with the local musicians, and the crowd went wild. Anthony was fun, exciting, and talented, and Rebecca didn't understand why he seemed so reserved when she first met him. She glimpsed into his soul the night he talked about high school prom. His experiences must have caused him to hold back and doubt himself. Once he felt comfortable with himself, he was fascinating. He was also an open book, easy to read and seduce, and that made the relationship simple since her preference was to be uncomplicated. They both detested playing games and were interested in a sure thing. It was simple; they just wanted to be together.

Early Friday morning, she was asleep in his arms when they heard a commotion downstairs. They looked outside and saw a black sedan parked on the street at 4 am. Rebecca saw Mrs. Grilli leaving the house, and she was crying. She observed Mr. Grilli for the first time, though a dark hoodie concealed his face. He appeared younger than she had imagined. Rebecca wanted to go to Mrs. Grilli to see what was wrong, but Anthony held her back.

"I don't think we are supposed to see this, Rebecca," he warned. "It's probably best if we pretend we are sleeping."

It took a few minutes for the Grillis to move their suitcases into the sedan, then the vehicle left. Rebecca was upset and too restless to sleep. He comforted her, then made love to her, and they stayed in bed until early morning. Finally, they moved to the kitchen for breakfast. At 8:30 they heard a soft knock on the door. Ellen. They had just seen her at the jazz club; something was amiss.

"Hi Anthony, Rebecca, I'm sorry to bother you, but Mrs. Capalini is hysterical and talking to us in Italian."

"I'm not able to speak very well," replied Anthony, "but I understand quite a bit. My grandparents on my dad's side were first-generation immigrants, and I spent many hours with them when I was young. I haven't used Italian for years."

"Would you come talk to Mrs. Capalini?"

"Of course."

Anthony was sitting at the kitchen table in his boxers and turned a bright shade of red. Ellen gave him an amused smile and looked him over to add to his discomfort. "I'm sorry to intrude when you are in your underwear, but I will be a physician in a few months and have seen everything."

"Right, Ellen."

Both girls thought he was cute.

***

Mrs. Capalini, enchanted by Anthony as he spoke to her in Italian, finally calmed down. She held a letter in Italian, and he translated most of it. The letter was a goodbye note from Mrs. Grilli to Mrs. Capalini. Anthony tried to surmise what had happened after reading the letter and considering what transpired early that morning. Ellen, Donna, and Rebecca were on the edge of their seats, wondering what this was about.

"It turns out," he started, "that the Grillis led a secret life, and that was not their real name. They were in a witness protection program; Mr. Grilli was a witness in a highly publicized case. They were not married, but Mrs. Grilli was not at liberty to discuss the nature of their relationship. Mrs. Grilli wrote that Mrs. Capalini was the best friend she ever had. She would miss her terribly, but they could never see each other again. She told Mrs. Capalini not to speak of her and that she should even burn her letters. Mrs. Grill explained she was always concerned about the safety of others, and that is why they kept to themselves. She was sorry to put anyone in danger. She asked for prayers and said she would always have fond memories of their friendship, which was honest and real."

"Oh my God," said Donna. "I always thought of Mr. Grilli as disabled or disfigured, and that is why we never saw him."

"We looked out the window at 4 am," said Rebecca, "and saw Mr. Grilli. He seemed fit and even younger than Mrs. Grilli, though we could not see his face and have no idea who he is."

They were silent for a few minutes. Finally, Ellen put the situation into perspective. "It doesn't matter who they are, or what happened in the past. They were nice neighbors, and Mrs. Capalini lost her best friend. It is up to us to comfort her."

All the attention had a calming effect on Mrs. Capalini. She had a sparkle in her eyes when she took Anthony's hand, then Rebecca's, and put their hands together with hers. "Nice boy ... nice girl," she said in a move that seemed to sanction their relationship. Anthony wondered to himself if Mrs. Capalini had matchmaking skills. She could have a power from the old country. Was this destiny? He hoped so. He doubted he could find a better match.

Chapter 26

Anthony could not believe the Easter break was over. In a short time, his relationship with Rebecca had become close, and it seemed like they had tried to condense six months of dating into six days because they knew their time together was short and precious. Rebecca would move in 2 months. They felt an overwhelming need to be together, but the demands of dental school would keep them apart for most of that time.

Rebecca attended Mass at St. Michael's Church on Sunday night, a short walk from her apartment. Anthony asked if he could go with her that Sunday after Easter.

"Of course, Anthony," she responded; "I would love to go to church with you." Rebecca hoped God would see how much they loved each other and that they would end up together as partners for life. Going to church with Anthony felt significant because they had a similar religious background and beliefs, and there was hope that a strong faith would help them find a way forward. The church at Saint Michael's was welcoming, and the congregation was made up of young families and college students. Three undergraduate women were leading in song for the first time. They had offered their talents when they realized the 7 pm Mass hd no cantor. Their harmonies were enchanting, and they sounded angelic. As they started singing a special arrangement after Communion, there was a hush in the church; their sound was magnificent. Rebecca felt a sudden sense of joy and well-being while experiencing the song, and when Anthony squeezed her hand, she knew he felt it too. The congregation was silent when the song ended; the parishioners moved in awe of the moment. And then something happened that rarely occurs at a Catholic Mass. There was applause and a standing ovation. The parishioners barely heard Father Andrew's closing prayer, and the applause subsided only when the cantors started the recessional hymn. Anthony and Rebecca were deep in thought as they walked to the apartment. Anthony finally broke the silence.

"Did something just happen in there?"

"If you are asking if that is the usual 7 pm Mass, the answer is no."

"It was inspirational. The music was moving; it seemed like divine intervention. I should go to confession and start going to church every week."

Rebecca took his hand and smiled. "We both need to go to confession, Anthony."

After a long pause, he said what she was thinking. "I know the church teaches that we should wait until marriage. It's hard to understand how it's wrong to give yourself to someone you care about."

"I know Anthony. But I don't think we'll burn in hell, but maybe spend some time in purgatory."

"I'll take my chances then," he said.

***

When Anthony returned to classes, he focused and accomplished more because he wanted time to spend with Rebecca. The amount of material he had to learn by the end of the year was staggering. Rebecca tried to limit their time together to Friday night and Saturday, then Anthony left on Sunday morning and returned for Mass at night. She did not want to distract him or interfere with his schoolwork. But Rebecca interfered on the day Dr. Hall confronted her. He stepped in her path, and she had no choice but to talk to him.

"Good day, Ms. Monahan."

"Dr. Hall."

"I see your freshman boyfriend is having problems with my courses. I may have to keep him here for summer school, or perhaps he won't return at all."

Dr. Hall hit a raw nerve. Rebecca was still heartsick that her study partner had flunked out freshman year because of Dr. Hall's classes. "I'm sure Anthony will be fine," countered Rebecca, "because he's studying from my notes, and I got a C in your classes. He is also putting in more time than I did. I'm sure he will pass."

"Those are strong predictions, Ms. Monahan. I don't know how you can be so sure about him when you were unsure of yourself as a freshman."

"I am sure of this, Dr. Hall. Toying with your students and playing God with their grades is unacceptable. I will request an audit of your grading system if you have targeted Anthony or any other freshman. This cat-and-mouse game you play by taunting your students has got to stop."

Dr. Hall was at first surprised by her fiery response but answered her with a mocking smile. "And what makes you think you have the authority to request such an audit?"

"Let's just say I usually mind my own business, but I know why Judy and Mia left last December. I overheard them talking about you. I'm sure Dean Gallagher would be unhappy about a scandal at this school."

For once, Dr. Hall seemed stunned and concerned. "Is that a threat, Ms. Monahan?"

"No, just a fact. As I said before, I try to mind my own business."

She didn't tell Anthony about her run-in with Dr. Hall. She remembered how angry he looked the day he interrupted them with the vacuum. The last thing Anthony needed was a fistfight with the anatomy professor.

Later that day, a visitor approached Dr. Bloom while Rebecca worked at her desk. The man had a German accent and seemed to hide from her as he walked out of the third-floor office. Then she saw his left hand and recognized it. He was the would-be intruder who pushed her while on the staircase. She called Pinkish and asked him to scope out the parking lot.

"Pinkish, see if that guy gets into a car, and see if you recognize it."

Pinkish ran to his vantage point on the skywalk. The car belonged to the intruder. They told Dr. Bloom.

"I think he's the man who tried to break in," she reported. "I recognized his hand, and Pinkish recognized the car he got into."

"How in the world did you recognize his hand?" asked Dr. Bloom.

"Well, I didn't want to say anything, but I was disturbed by it. He has thick black hair on his wrists and knuckles. I think he should look into electrolysis. The plain gold wedding band looked familiar. Who was he?"

"He is from a German company interested in my bleaching research."

"Well, don't trust him. He's looking to steal your formula!"

Dr. Bloom seemed unconcerned.

"I doubt that, Rebecca. It is common knowledge that certain peroxide combinations will bleach teeth. An orthodontist discovered it by accident when treating a patient for gingivitis. The patient's gums were hyperplastic, so he made trays for the patient to wear and instructed him to put a peroxide gel in them. It not only helped his gingivitis; his teeth turned several shades lighter."

"Well, the bleach worked on me," said Rebecca.

"I think it was the dispenser he was interested in," observed Dr. Bloom. "A patent is pending on it. I will give you details in the future."

***

Mr. Marlow called Dean Gallagher to set up a meeting. Dr. Bloom had called him with the name of the German company and the representative, and Marlow did some digging. "I'm happy to report," said Marlow, "that we can tie up some loose ends. I checked out the company represented by the German man who visited you, Dr. Bloom. The company exists despite accusations of stealing intellectual property from research groups. I suggest you avoid contact with that company in the future."

"Were they responsible for the break-ins?" asked the dean.

"I believe so, but there is no way to prove it. If the school is involved in cutting-edge research, discussions should be confidential."

"Is that all?" asked the dean.

"I do not think we will ever know what happened to the missing opioids last year. I suspect it was a student or employee no longer here, or possibly theft from your previous cleaning service. Regardless, there is no longer a problem since there have been no attempts this year. I also investigated the cadaver with the head injury. It seems the medical school was short on donors and let him slip through. The man was a World War II veteran who had an injury from the war."

"That's a relief," said the dean. "I had visions of an attempt to hide a crime through the donation process."

"No, nothing like that."

The dean was still feeling anxious. "Anything else?"

"I'm afraid I have some information about the employees who left in December. It seems Dr. Hall's former assistant, Mia Reynolds, is about to give birth. She claims Dr. Hall is the father and plans to file a paternity suit. Judy Jones witnessed the affair and was disgusted by Dr. Hall's refusal to take responsibility. Then she quit ."

"I was afraid it was something like that," said the dean. "The school is turning into Peyton Place. I just heard a rumor that a senior will elope with one of the instructors after the graduation ceremony."

"Don't take it to heart," said Marlow. "It's not a reflection on the school, just on life. I imagine your job has gotten more complicated since they started admitting women to the school."

"You can say that. I am not accustomed to students weeping in my office. But this is a stressful environment, and if a female student has an occasional meltdown, it is not such a bad coping mechanism."

"It sure beats a fight or a duel!" joked Marlow.

Mr. Marlow was aware that Rebecca's downstairs neighbor had been a witness in a high-level corruption case. He told the dean that for a time he wondered if Rebecca was a target just because she lived upstairs. However, the matter was unrelated to the school and was no longer an issue since they relocated the witness. The dean put his hand on his head. He was getting a headache and was ready for the school year to end.

***

The final days before graduation passed quickly. Rebecca told her parents about her change of plans; rather than helping her move out after graduation, they were planning to fly out for the weekend and then return to New Jersey. They were disappointed she would not be able to come home but were still proud to be at the graduation. She would have to return alone at the end of June, taking only what fit in her little red Mustang.

Chapter 27

On a rainy Friday night, Anthony drove Rebecca to her apartment. She had anxiety about safety in the neighborhood, and he had been staying with her more often. She was uncomfortable being alone in the house without downstairs tenants. The forecast was for rain all weekend, so their only plans included getting pizza on Friday night and studying on Sunday. Rebecca softened her resolve about limiting their time together since he could focus on his studies while staying with her at her apartment. She was always concerned about his demanding schedule.

"Anthony, I spoke to Mrs. Capalini yesterday, and she asked if you are interested in leasing the Grilli's place. It is a fully furnished two-bedroom apartment. The Grillis left most of their belongings behind so you wouldn't have to buy a thing."

"I am interested; let's reach out to Mrs. Capalini tomorrow. Chuck has been a fun roommate, but now that he is dating Ellen, I am sure he would appreciate his privacy. I also know Pinkish needs a place for next year."

"That's perfect. Mrs. Capalini worries about renting to students she doesn't know. She never advertises, it has always been through referral."

Anthony considered it advantageous to everyone involved. "I think Mrs. Capalini will need someone to help her once you girls move out."

"Well, she adores you, Anthony. Maybe you can brush up on your Italian."

"There is that. By the way, Rebecca, one of your colleagues was talking about you yesterday."

"Really? Anything good?"

"It was Jeff Muller, and to tell you the truth, I'm a little jealous."

"How could you be? I haven't seen him since the day he assisted in my wisdom tooth surgery."

"His comments were about that day. He told me about your tori; says they're quite remarkable."

"What! He's not supposed to disclose personal information about a patient."

"The conversation was amusing, and I'm sure he meant no offense. He didn't think you would mind. Can I see them?"

"Believe me, Anthony, it's not my best feature. When we practiced injections on each other, our instructor noticed. I had to expose them to the entire team."

"So half the guys in your class have seen them, and I'm your boyfriend and I haven't?"

"Anthony, you have seen more of me than anyone on earth. I think you can skip the tori."

He was quiet, and she didn't know if he was joking or upset. He, of course, was teasing her.

" Anthony, the mouth mirror is in the medicine cabinet. I swear, you're such a freak."

He gently examined Rebecca. Her anatomy explained the soft snoring he occasionally heard when sleeping with her. He didn't want her to feel bad about herself, so he attempted an awkward compliment.

"You have the best tori around."

"Shut up, Anthony."

He chuckled at her fiery response and continued to tease her. "If I were to write a poem, what would rhyme with torus? I know, chorus."

"Anthony, you are such a weirdo. No wonder you ended up in dental school."

After a moment, they both laughed. Not many students chose to pursue this profession; you would have to be dedicated to it and have an offbeat sense of humor. Anthony had both. And of course, all of this teasing led to sex, but their interactions usually led them there. They were both under stress at school, and being together was their escape. When they were alone, they couldn't keep their hands off each other. Now Rebecca could say that Anthony had seen everything. But they still had so much to learn about each other. Anthony was tight-lipped about his past, and she suspected he had disappointments with women that were far more devastating than his high school prom fiasco. His self-deprecating humor was more than an act. Anthony was handsome, smart, talented, and a phenomenal lover. There was no reason for him to lack self-confidence, yet he did. She wanted to help him overcome his insecurities. She made a clumsy attempt to build him up.

"Anthony, you are so powerful and passionate, I look at you as an exciting adventurer or a Greek god."

He didn't know where that came from but was instantly amused. He decided to participate in the fantasy since he knew where it was heading.

"You make me feel like one Rebecca. But then again, you are the siren who has power over me. Although you think of me in such an intriguing way, I am merely a mortal."

She smiled. He didn't take her seriously. "But I have no power unless we are at sea."

"I'm begging you to lure me to the ocean; I don't care if I never come back."

Anthony listened to the pouring rain and realized he would forever think of her when he was on the lake or at the ocean. He took her on that rainy night until they were both satisfied and exhausted. As he stroked her hair, he heard a gentle snore. He knew she felt safe in his arms.

In the morning, Anthony looked at the invitation. He has to RSVP for a wedding he felt obligated to attend. The day would be tolerable if Rebecca agreed to go with him.

"Rebecca, my roommate from college is getting married on June 21st, and you will still be in town. Would you be my date?"

"Do you want me there, Anthony?"

"Of course. I can't imagine having any fun without you."

"Well yes, I'm glad I will still be here and would love to go to the wedding with you. Would you like to come to my graduation?"

Anthony sighed. He didn't think he belonged at the graduation. "Listen, Rebecca, I am so proud of you and would love to see you graduate. But I think it is a special moment for you and your parents, and a farewell to your class, so I don't think I should go. It wouldn't be right to meet your parents and then not see them again."

She knew he was right but didn't want to think about not seeing him again. Her mom wouldn't understand her having a boyfriend whom she would leave behind.

" Besides," he added, "your graduation is right before finals week; I will need the time to study."

" I understand, Anthony."

What she didn't understand was his reluctance to go to his roommate's wedding. Perhaps he would tell her in time.

Chapter 28

Graduation was for the entire school, including undergraduates and professional students. Because it was a big event, most hotels were booked for the weekend. When Mrs. Capalini heard the Monahans were having trouble finding a room nearby, she offered the Grilli's place to them. Rebecca cleaned the apartment before they arrived. When Rebecca picked her parents up at the airport, they were pleased with the accommodations and happy that Rebecca was upstairs and her car was convenient. Her mother busied herself with food shopping, and Rebecca had time to talk to her dad about her plans and hopes for the future. They enjoyed spending time together and preparing for graduation day. The ceremony itself was long, and Rebecca's class did not stay to celebrate afterward. They all went their separate ways with their families. Fortunately, she had made plans with Anna, Ellen, and Donna to celebrate with the parents at a local steakhouse.

"Well, this is wonderful," commented Rebecca's dad. "Two dentists, a doctor, and a lawyer, all beautiful young ladies starting their careers."

But Rebecca's mom was disappointed in her daughter. She had not found a professional man to marry.

"Are you girls all single?" she asked.

"We are all dating someone," replied Donna.

"Rebecca, you didn't tell us you were seeing someone," pried her mother.

"I am. He's a great guy, but has three more years of dental school, and I am leaving."

She waited for her mother's disapproval. "Why couldn't you find someone in your class?" she asked.

Rebecca tried to curb her resentment. Having a mother who thought marrying a dentist was more important than being a dentist was frustrating. She wondered how her mother would feel if Anthony was the janitor he first seemed to be. Rebecca was skeptical about living at home with her in New Jersey and had second thoughts. After that tense moment, the other parents took over the conversation, and the evening was fun and festive. Everyone was in good spirits, and they all had a good time. The hard part was saying goodbye to Anna, who was leaving for California in the morning and taking the California boards in a few weeks. Rebecca wondered when she would see her again.

When she brought her parents to the airport the following day, her mother continued to pump her for information about Anthony.

"Is he Irish?"

"No, Italian."

Another disappointment. "When did you meet him?"

"I met him at the beginning of the year, but recently we grew close. He is a wonderful guy, but we haven't had enough time together to commit. He has three more years to finish dental school."

"Well, why did you even start anything?" asked her mother.

Rebecca sighed. "It started as just friends, Mom." There was no way she could make her mother understand. The woman didn't have a romantic bone in her body. She wondered how her mother had attracted a great guy like her dad.

***

With graduation over, Rebecca had to return to the clinic to finish her requirements. One glaring deficiency was in the periodontal department. She was adept at scaling and root planing but had not completed a periodontal surgery. She was not interested in doing these surgeries when in private practice and wished she could skip the requirement. Two seniors returned to the clinic after graduation, and Rebecca was one of them. She felt out-of-place joining the third-year students, and Rebecca no longer felt like she belonged. It was time to wrap up her dental school career.

Anthony had a miserable exam week. His work-study was over since the school hired a professional service for the summer. He didn't see Rebecca or work with Pinkish all week. The hours were filled with exams and study; there was no other diversion. He missed Rebecca, but they had plans for the Friday after his exams. The entire student body and faculty were finishing the curriculum in time for summer break.

***

Dean Gallagher held meetings during the week. The professors had time to schedule a year-end meeting with the dean while the students took exams. The dean dreaded his appointment with Dr. Hall but knew the situation had to be discussed. When Dr. Hall entered the dean's office, he was subdued and looked disheveled. Dean Gallagher's approach softened.

"Dr. Hall, I have become aware of your situation, and I think we should talk about it."

" Did Rebecca tell you what happened?" he asked.

"Rebecca? Rebecca Monahan? What does she have to do with it?" asked the dean.

"Nothing, really. She was simply aware of what was going on."

"No, she did not say anything. My information is from Mr. Marlow. He did a background check on all employees frequenting the third-floor offices. He indicated that Ms. Reynolds has a lawyer."

"Is the school facing a sexual harassment suit?" asked Hall.

"No, and it doesn't seem she is pursuing that route. It seems to be a personal matter between you and Ms. Reynolds."

Dr. Hall was reluctant to discuss his personal life, but knew he must. He started at the beginning. "My marriage has been unhappy for a long time, and after Ms. Reynolds and I worked so many hours together, our relationship became intimate. After ten years of a childless marriage, I was evaluated at a fertility clinic and told it was unlikely I could father a child. I was distressed and ashamed of my condition. What I have since found out is that my wife didn't want children and had secretly been taking precautions all along. When Ms. Reynolds approached me with her situation, I thought she was lying; I couldn't believe I was a father. But now that I have seen the extreme measures she has taken to hold me accountable, I realize she is telling the truth. Mia is a quiet girl; she spent so much time with me that I can't imagine her being with another man during those months. I plan to get a divorce and live up to my responsibilities as a father. I don't know if I can patch my relationship with Mia, but I will try. I am also handing in my resignation and hope you will give me a reference."

"Of course," said the dean." You understand that we don't intend to dismiss you. This is purely a personal matter."

But Dr. Hall had decided and had chosen his path. "I want to find a position at the undergraduate level. I don't enjoy interacting with the students, and as an undergraduate professor, I can rely on teaching assistants to monitor the labs and tutor the students. I have grown weary of these dental students constantly challenging me."

"What do you mean?" asked the dean.

"Well, take Mr. Roselli, for instance."

"Anthony Roselli? He is one of the most level-headed students in the school!"

"Not when defending Ms. Monahan. Once I asked her to assist with some paperwork, and when Mr. Roselli intervened, I got the impression he wanted to deck me."

Dean Gallagher couldn't believe what he was hearing.

Dr. Hall continued. "Ms. Monahan is another one; she is a tigress when defending Mr. Roselli. She threatened me and told me she would demand an audit of my grading system if she suspected bias. I want to wash my hands of the entire semester. A teaching assistant will evaluate the final exams and calculate the final grades. I have been hard on certain students, but I was only trying to toughen them up. I certainly did not mean to target them, and I suppose my sometimes unpleasant demeanor was because I was so unhappy with myself."

"I see," said the dean. He called Mrs. Susman into his office. "Marjorie; please open the cabinet."

Mrs. Susman complied with a wide-eyed nod. "Do you want your refreshment in here?"

"Yes please, and bring another glass."

Dean Gallagher rarely took a drink of his special scotch during school hours. He usually indulged late on a Friday afternoon. Mrs. Susman wondered what had happened. She poured drinks for Dean Gallagher and Dr. Hall.

***

Anthony and Pinkish were called to the dean's office the following day. They were nervous about their academic standing, though it was too soon to be about final grades. Dr. Bloom, Dean Gallagher, Anthony, and Pinkish took a seat in the dean's office.

"We are waiting for another student," said the dean.

The four men stood when Rebecca walked in. She smiled at Anthony and Pinkish because she thought she knew what the meeting was about and wanted to put their minds at ease. Dr. Bloom spoke first.

"Please examine the object in front of you." They all examined the plastic dispenser, which was double-barreled with a plunger and a mixing tip that screwed on, and the tip had little swirls of plastic within it.

"This," said Dr. Bloom proudly, " is the patented item and the probable cause of the break-ins."

The students looked at the dispenser. They did not appreciate the significance of what they were looking at, but Dr. Bloom and Dean Gallagher were excited as Dr. Bloom tried to explain. "We have always had to rely on assistants to mix properly, and the materials are technique sensitive. If the assistant does not mix Impregum with a heavy hand, you will get air bubbles in your impression. If zinc phosphate cement is not slowly and carefully mixed on a cool glass slab, your cement will set up too quickly and the crown will not fully seat. Or worse yet, if the acid component does not neutralize with proper mixing, the patient may experience sensitivity. But this mixing device will change dentistry and make it easier. The assistant will simply have to attach the tip to the double-barrel plunger, and the material will combine in the tip portion. Right now I am using this system for whitening gel. But the application could be used for many of our current materials and materials that will be developed in the future."

The students were happy for Dr. Bloom but did not appreciate the enormity of this breakthrough.

"Does this mean you won't be teaching dental materials next year?" asked Anthony.

"I will be here. The plastic company owns the patent, and it may be a few years before I can fully appreciate the financial stability this patent will provide me. I expect to teach next year, and Anthony and Pinkish, you will be my students."

Anthony looked at Rebecca. He was exhausted and emotional about the crazy year that was about to end. She knew he needed sleep and took the initiative to end the meeting.

"I am excited about your success, Dr. Bloom. Thank you for sharing it with us. I think the freshmen are tired, and they need some rest."

Dean Gallagher looked from Anthony to Rebecca. Now he saw what had been there all along. Perhaps the most surprising story of the year was the quiet and reserved Anthony Roselli capturing the heart of the vivid and beautiful Rebecca Monahan. She was a surprise too. She looked like a model and didn't seem tough enough to get through four years of dental school. But here she was on her way to her chosen profession. And the dean could foresee Mr. Roselli getting his degree in three years. He felt sorry for them because he couldn't see how their relationship could persevere. He wished them the best.

Chapter 29

Anthony's exams ended on Friday, and Rebecca planned out their Friday night. They would meet at her apartment, she would prepare dinner, and then he could shower or take a relaxing bath, and catch up on his sleep. But when he arrived, there was one thing he needed most. Her. She brought him into her room and told him to relax, then asked him to close his eyes and to forget his brutal exam week. She urged him to leave everything to her and promised she would take care of him; all he had to do was surrender. The suggestion was very erotic. Anthony was exhausted, and she was gentle and loving and gave him what he needed. He had the energy to make sure she was satisfied, and they had another epic adventure in each other's arms. She insisted he eat a light dinner, and then he slept. She wasn't tired but lay beside him, savoring thoughts of the next few weeks together and dreading the reality of their time limit.

Rebecca's mind raced as she considered three scenarios. She thought it was crazy to consider staying with him after a very short whirlwind romance. He was only 22 years old and could change during the three years, and she would smother him, locking up his future at a young age. He would still be a student, and they would occupy two different worlds. She feared that staying would ruin what they had. If she moved to New Jersey, they could have a long-distance romance. But when she tried that with Kyle, the loneliness and resentment caused the end of the relationship. She could see a long-distance courtship surviving a year at most; three years was much too long. This brought her to the last option, which, though heartbreaking, was probably for the best. She would leave at the end of June. With no choice in the matter, he would have to let her go and could not blame himself. The decision would be hers, and she would be the one to have regrets. He could then be free to find the right partner when he was older and ready for it, and their passionate affair would be a beautiful memory they would always have. She had to do this for Anthony. She loved him with all her heart and needed to do what was right for him; what was right for both of them. With a heavy ache in her chest, she fell asleep beside him.

In the morning, she smelled coffee brewing and heard the shower running. How she wished every day could be like this. He shaved and emerged looking rested and refreshed.

"Thank you for last night. Rebecca, you were amazing."

She smiled. She caught a whiff of his aftershave, and the spicy scent roused her imagination. "Anytime Anthony. It felt like you came from a battle on the high seas."

"Only to be conquered by the most beautiful siren," he added.

"How do you think you did on your exams?"

" I may have passed them all. I am in a slightly better position than last semester, and I hear Dr. Hall will not be in charge of grading. That guy hates me."

"He is just challenged by you, Anthony. You are the stronger man."

He thought maybe Rebecca was right, and felt sorry for Dr. Hall. "How about you, Rebecca; how are your requirements?"

"I still need to do periodontal surgery. Unfortunately, none of my patients have been surgical candidates."

"Is a frenectomy considered periodontal surgery?"

"I guess so. Do you know anyone who needs a frenectomy?"

"Yes, me."

"I know what you're thinking ... absolutely not, Anthony. I will not perform a surgery I know nothing about on you."

"But I trust you, and the instructor will tell you what to do."

"The answer is no."

***

When she arrived at the clinic on Tuesday morning, she was told she had a new patient. She approached the woman at the front desk. "What were you thinking?" she asked. "I'm leaving in a few weeks and should not be assigned a new patient."

"But he asked for you specifically," retorted the receptionist.

When handed the chart, she read the name, Anthony Mark Roselli. He was in the waiting area.

"What are you doing here, Anthony?"

"Dr. Kudlow examined me yesterday and agreed I should have the frenectomy. He put me on your schedule."

Rebecca brought Anthony to the periodontal department. She approached the instructor. "Dr. Kudlow; Anthony is my boyfriend, and I don't think it's appropriate that I perform this surgery."

Dr. Kudlow was adamant. "He wants the surgery, he needs the surgery, and you need the requirement. I will walk you through the procedure, and when you are done, I will sign you off on your periodontal credits. A lower labial frenectomy to prevent further recession is indicated. It is a minor procedure and should prevent the need for a graft in the future. Administer the lidocaine, and I will let you know what instruments to get out."

Anthony had a big smile on his face.

"You wouldn't smile if you knew what I am going to do to you."

"Oh, really? I am well-versed in the procedure. I could do it myself with a mirror."

"You truly are a weirdo, Anthony."

The procedure was not lengthy. Rebecca ordered him to avoid lifting since she suspected he might want to move into the Grilli's apartment. Anthony drove home, and since he should rest after his surgery, he had a book from the library to entertain him, a romance novel. The story was different, but the plot was the same — imperfect hero and beautiful girl, thrown together by circumstances that led to a steamy and passionate affair. He escaped into the book. He was feeling frisky, a little sore but well-rested and relaxed. The romance novel made him feel romantic, and the surgery did not deter his libido. He drove to Rebecca's place for dinner; she was heating soup when he walked in. He passed through the kitchen and went to her room to lie down. Rebecca followed.

"Anthony, are you feeling sore?"

"Not really."

"What are you doing, Anthony?"

"Is there something on the stove? Turn it off and come back. I need some sympathy."

She turned off the stove and returned.

"Come here, Rebecca."

She knew where this was leading. "Anthony, be quiet, be still, and don't smile. I don't want anything to happen to your sutures."

"Don't worry. If anything happens to me, my dentist is right here."

He enjoyed it when she took charge. The attention she gave him was so sensual, so carnal, the hard part for him was to refrain from smiling. He imagined smiling for years when he thought about it. He was grateful to have a few normal weeks with Rebecca. They had conducted a most passionate love affair under hostile circumstances. Now they had time to make the most of every minute. They tried not to think about what would happen next since Rebecca was firm in her resolve to return to New Jersey.

Chapter 30

Rebecca needed a dress for the wedding, so she asked Ellen to go shopping with her. Anthony's friends and family would be there, and she wanted to make a good impression. The dresses she tried on were conservative and ordinary, and she was disappointed because she was hoping for something more flattering. Ellen then picked up a dress Rebecca would not have considered, and when she emerged from the dressing room, Ellen smiled brightly. "Rebecca, that dress was made for you."

"But Ellen, this dress is hot. His parents will be there."

"I think it's appropriate," observed Ellen. "Just a little cleavage showing and the skirt falls below the knee. It's classy. The aquamarine silk is stunning."

"But the dress is form-fitting, and the slit in the skirt is high and provocative."

"You are not Rebecca of Sunnybrook Farm," Ellen scolded. "Anthony would love to show off his sexy girlfriend at the wedding. You look so attractive when you get dressed up and put on makeup; he will be proud to have you as his date."

After some thought, Rebecca realized the only person she should be concerned about pleasing was Anthony, and she should wear a dress that made her look classy and sexy; someone Anthony was proud to date. She felt quite glamorous in the dress. She bought matching high heels and jewelry and purchased an aquamarine silk tie for him.

***

As Rebecca peered out her window, she saw Anthony, who looked dashing in a grey suit and the silk tie that matched her dress. Her heart skipped a beat when she opened her door to greet him. She thought he might fall off the landing when he saw her.

"Thank you, God," he whispered.

"Do you like the dress?"

"There is no way to describe the effect you have on me. I can't believe I'm the lucky guy taking you out tonight."

Rebecca grabbed her overnight bag, since they had a hotel room a few blocks from the reception. Because there was an open bar, they didn't want to worry about driving back. She draped a shawl over her shoulders as she felt self-conscious wearing her sexy dress in church. Carmen and Matt were married in a small Catholic church close to the reception hall. Carmen was petite, with dark hair and an Italian background, and Matt was tall and blond. They were a handsome couple. Anthony and Rebecca stood in line to congratulate them after the ceremony. Rebecca noticed Anthony was tense; polite but not the warm smiling guy she expected at his college roommate's wedding. Something seemed wrong to her. He relaxed during the drive to the reception and cocktail hour. Rebecca met Anthony's family. She caught Tommy giving Anthony a thumbs-up when they thought she wasn't looking. His sister Angela was talkative and friendly. His father was all smiles and having a fun time, and his Aunt Edith was outspoken and colorful. Only his mother seemed reserved, and Rebecca worried the dress was too sexy for his mother's taste. She had to remind herself that the dress was for Anthony, and if Mrs. Roselli had any idea how much Rebecca cared for her son, she would warm up to her. Anthony offered to get drinks for Rebecca and Aunt Edith. When alone, Aunt Edith smiled at Rebecca and squeezed her hand.

"Don't tell the others, but Anthony is my favorite nephew. He seems so happy to be with you tonight. Have you been dating long?"

"We met at the beginning of the school year, but have been dating for a few months."

"Well, if you're smart, you'll hang on to him. He's a good catch."

"I know Aunt Edith. He's amazing."

"Not everyone sees what we see. I probably shouldn't say anything, but Carmen and Anthony dated in college, and the family hoped for a match. But somehow she ended up with his roommate. She has never been my cup of tea. I think Anthony is a good sport to be here tonight."

"Thank you for telling me, Aunt Edith. I will give Anthony special attention."

"Good girl," said Aunt Edith as she finished another gin and tonic and gave Rebecca a wink.

Rebecca understood the situation. She did everything she could to boost his ego. She stayed close to him and didn't let go of him, whether dancing with him, holding his hand, or embracing him in a private moment.

She knows, thought Anthony. *Aunt Edith must have said something.* In a way, he was relieved since he was certain she sensed an awkwardness and did not want Rebecca to think it had anything to do with her. His heart melted as she showered him with attention.

It made him love her even more. They danced the night away, and Rebecca realized she had been right about Anthony at the dental school prom; he had ballroom skills. He was a strong lead and knew how to showcase his partner. She hoped the slit in her dress did not shock the relatives when he dipped her. Although his dance moves were not inappropriate, they were seductive and seemed like a prelude to spending the night with her in the hotel room. Toward the end of the reception, Mrs. Roselli approached Rebecca.

"I am concerned about Anthony driving," she said. "He usually has only one or two drinks, but tonight he overdid it; he shouldn't drive."

"It's not a problem, Mrs. Roselli. I have been drinking ginger ale for the last two hours and will drive. We have a room nearby." She could tell his mother disapproved of their plans but was relieved her son wouldn't be driving. She looked at Rebecca and tried to see what was in her heart.

"Anthony has told us so much about you, and I am glad you are here with him tonight. But he also tells us you're leaving."

"That's right, I am headed for New Jersey in two weeks. I know Anthony still has a long way to go to finish school, and I know what it's like. I will miss him terribly when I leave." She couldn't control the tears that welled up and made every effort to control her emotions.

Mrs. Roselli took her hand and looked into the bright aquamarine eyes that told her everything. "Rebecca, I do like you."

***

Rebecca had never seen Anthony drunk, but was sure he was. He looked glassy-eyed and grew silent. After the cake had been served,

Rebecca asked Anthony if they could leave. They said goodbye to Mr. and Mrs. Roselli and exited. Under the circumstances, they didn't feel obligated to say goodbye to the bride and groom before they left. Rebecca got behind the wheel as promised, and they drove to the hotel.

"Thank you for the ride, Rebecca." He smiled as they approached the hotel. "Thank you for your beautiful dress, your gorgeous smile, your pretty hair..."

" You don't have to thank me, Anthony; I'm just happy to be with you tonight."

She guided him into the hotel room and took off his tie. She hung up his suit jacket and led him to the bed, removing his shoes and socks, expecting he might pass out. But he took off his trousers and pulled her toward him. After she slipped off her dress, she submitted to him. The experience was raw, lustful, and intense as she yielded to him. He was so forceful that it surprised her. It also aroused her, and she found it so stimulating she thought she could scream. But it ended a little too soon for her, and he left her wound up and craving more. He moved to his side of the bed, and she thought he would drift into a deep sleep.

Rebecca doubted she could sleep. He left her frustrated, and Anthony's forceful behavior surprised her. She remembered the day at the lake and how he seemed to submit to her, but tonight he was in charge, an alpha male, so strong and masculine, unapologetic and bursting with testosterone. She saw a different facet of Anthony as he continued to be full of surprises. With a sigh, she closed her eyes and tried to get some sleep. After a few minutes, she felt him snuggle up behind her.

"Rebecca, are you asleep?" he whispered.

"No, Anthony, I'm awake."

"I'm sorry," he said gently. "I guess I was acting like a caveman."

"Don't apologize; I liked it ... I like you."

He held her a little tighter. He was so warm and close as he whispered from behind. "I guess you spoke to Aunt Edith tonight."

"I did. She told me about you and Carmen."

"I think I should explain."

"You don't have to tell me if you don't want to."

He paused. "I don't want you to think I still have feelings for her because I don't. But it was hard to get past the betrayal."

She waited for him to continue and wondered if he would.

"The thing is," he started, "I thought I might be in love with her, but now that I know what love is, I'm sure I wasn't." He stroked Rebecca's hair and moved even closer before he continued. "Carmen is a cousin by marriage, and when our families realized we were going to the same college, they asked me to help her adjust. She was a freshman and a year behind me. I introduced her to my friends and comforted her when she was homesick. After a time, she made friends at school, and she no longer needed my help. We ran into each other after that, but our association was mostly as cousins, though she was not in my family until her mother's recent marriage. Our families encouraged us to date, so when I was a senior, I thought, why not? I was attracted to her, but we didn't become physically intimate. One day I had a double lab period that was canceled because of a mishap in the chemistry department. When I returned to the dorm room, I walked in on Carmen and Matt having sex. I quickly left and returned an hour later to move my belongings out of the dorm room. Matt tried to talk to me, but what could he say? They could have told me how they felt about each other, and I would have stepped aside. Instead, they were sneaking around behind my back, and I had to find out in the most brutal way. I always told myself I showed discretion afterward because I was protecting Carmen. The truth is, I was humiliated. She rejected me, then betrayed me, and I felt stupid and naïve. Our families think we ended the relationship amicably, and then she started dating Matt. Only three people knew the actual story. Now you know too."

Rebecca was glad he was behind her because she was sure he didn't want her pity, and she didn't know if she could hide it.

"Anthony, Aunt Edith knows something happened. She tried to tell me about Carmen, then asked me to take care of you and winked at me. In her way, she hinted you might have mixed feelings about the bride and groom."

"Aunt Edith could always read me like a book. I'm sure it didn't take much imagination for her to guess what had happened."

"You didn't have to go to that wedding, Anthony. It would have been their problem if the relatives wondered why you were not at the wedding. You shouldn't feel bad about yourself; you did nothing wrong."

"You're right, but I had to face the hurt again to let it go. I'm sorry I dragged you into this mess." His voice wavered before he made a raw and honest admission. "The thing is, I started to believe I was not passionate enough to satisfy a partner. Now I know I just hadn't found the right girl."

She clasped her hands over his. "I'm so glad we found each other. I didn't know the meaning of passion until I met you. You are the most romantic, thrilling man I have ever met ... don't change."

He seemed ready to fall asleep, but as he started to doze, he whispered, "Please stay with me."

Rebecca's heart skipped a beat. Each day he revealed more of himself, and the more she learned, the more love she felt for him. Finally, she thought she should tell him about the conversation with his mom.

"Anthony, your mother knows we are sleeping together. She was concerned about your driving, so I had to tell her about the room."

This comment awakened him. His mother was so straight-laced, he was sure she thought him a virgin. He didn't know what to say. He let reality sink in. "Well," he sighed, "since my parents and Aunt Edith probably noticed I couldn't keep my hands off you, and by now they all know where we are, we shouldn't waste the room."

He hadn't finished his sentence before she was all over him. Her enthusiasm turned him on. He never imagined a heart-to-heart talk would elicit this response. He knew very little about women.

***

They fell asleep exhausted and satisfied, and woke up in each other's arms the next morning. Rebecca took one look at Anthony and knew he was hungover. They dressed in comfortable clothes for the ride back, and Rebecca offered to drive. "I think we both need a nutritious breakfast. Maybe we can find a diner on the way back."

"Rebecca, we're not in New Jersey; there are no diners in this state. There is, however, a breakfast chain about 20 minutes down the road."

"Perfect."

When they entered the busy restaurant, he led her to a private booth in the back, and Rebecca assumed he needed quiet, but the truth is he wanted a private place to talk. She ordered two large glasses of ice water, gave him an aspirin, and the waitress brought a large glass of orange juice.

"I'm a little embarrassed about my behavior at the hotel. My only excuse is that I was drunk, and I seem to have lost all of my filters."

"I'm glad it happened, Anthony. We all have a past that somehow shapes us. Now I know yours."

"But I don't know about your past boyfriends, Rebecca."

"You never asked."

"I am asking now."

She sighed. "My mother always told me it was best to avoid talking about past boyfriends to someone you're dating. But what's fair is fair now that I know what happened to you. The truth is, there isn't much to tell. I was tall and skinny and somewhat awkward in high school, and my first date was my senior prom. I thought my date was nice when I said yes to the prom, but he expected something in return. Nothing bad happened, but I wasn't interested in him as a boyfriend and didn't want to hurt his feelings. I allowed him to kiss me just to be polite."

Anthony nearly choked on his orange juice.

"Are you okay?"

"Well, yes, I'm just a little dehydrated. Please continue."

"I dated in college and had fun, but nothing serious. Then, as a freshman in dental school, I met someone, but it was long distance and the relationship didn't work out. At first, I thought the distance ruined the relationship, but eventually, I realized he wasn't right for me. When he continued to send letters, I ended it. Then I had that awful experience with the guy who left me at the jazz club. He was married, but I didn't know it, and he left to avoid being caught cheating by his brother-in-law. That was only a first date, and that's the night you walked me home."

Anthony absorbed this information and concluded she probably wouldn't be open to continuing their courtship long-distance. He had no choice but to let her go if that's what she wanted. All he could do was enjoy the time they had left and say a little prayer that she might have a change of heart.

Part II

The Decision

Chapter 31

As the end of June approached, Rebecca finished her requirements. Mrs. Capalini found a tenant for Rebecca's apartment; it was Anthony's friend, Joe Reilly. He bought Rebecca's couch and TV, and she left her dishes, pots, and pans for him. She didn't have room in the Mustang for many belongings. Anthony had already moved to the downstairs apartment, so they spent their nights there until she was ready to leave. Only a few precious days remained. They sailed again and had dinner with Aunt Sophie and Uncle Mark. They hiked. Anthony took her to a Rick Derringer concert. They double-dated with Ellen and Chuck. But in the end, they ran out of time. The heartache had already started for both of them, and Anthony tried to talk about it.

"Rebecca, are you sure this is what you want?"

"What I want and what I can have are two different things, Anthony. You know I wish we could change our situation. We have to make the best decision considering our circumstances."

Anthony took a deep breath and made a bold statement. "Rebecca, I would marry you today if I thought you would have me."

She cried. "Anthony, we're not ready. We need to focus on careers right now. The timing is not right."

"So you're breaking up with me?"

"I'm letting you go. There is a difference."

"It feels the same," he said sadly.

And finally, it was time to say goodbye. She tried not to dwell on how it would happen. For years, men and women have had to say goodbye under dire circumstances; going off to war, a long absence, a fatal illness. This was not so tragic, and they had to put it into perspective.

"Anthony, please don't make this any harder for us. Help me make this move."

"As you wish," he responded with a sad smile. He helped her pack her car. He bought her snacks for the road and gave her pictures from the wedding. They shared one last desperate kiss before she got in the Mustang and drove off. When she looked in the rearview mirror, Anthony was hurrying toward his apartment. She thought he was crying.

She made it two blocks, and then she pulled over. She cried and cried, somehow pulled herself together, and headed east.

Chapter 32

His eyes blurred with tears. "She left me," he said out loud as if that would make it easier to believe. He wondered if she would change her mind and turn back, but in his heart, he knew that wouldn't happen. After all, this was the plan from the beginning, and she begged him to make it easier for her. He was devastated but had no choice but to respect her wishes. He needed physical work to distract him from the depression that was crushing him. The Grilli's apartment was gloomy with block-out drapes and dark walls, and the atmosphere matched his mood. The rooms were dreary, and Mrs. Grilli was shocked by how the apartment had changed through the years. She asked Anthony to paint and renovate and offered to pay him for his time. She chose a warm linen-white paint with ultra-white trim and asked that the entire apartment be done. Anthony suspected it would need primer and two coats to cover the walls. He was grateful for the project and worked until he was so tired he had to sleep. After he crashed into bed, he still had trouble falling asleep; he was used to sleeping by her side and missed her. Her pillow still carried the scent of fresh lemons from her hair conditioner. As he journeyed towards slumber, he would reach next to him to see if she was there and listen for the gentle snoring he had gotten used to. Then he awakened to silence and an empty pillow. Finally, exhausted and full of paint, he managed a troubled sleep.

Bright sunlight streamed through the bedroom window as he awakened, and for about five seconds he was happy to greet a new sunny day. But then, a stab in the heart when he realized she was gone, followed by a heavy crushing feeling in his chest that wouldn't go away. He wondered how long it would take to move past that lingering pain.

***

Rebecca had a tough road ahead of her. Her solitary drive back to New Jersey gave her too much time to think. She planned overnight stops visiting two college friends, one in Indiana and one in Pennsylvania. Instead of the fun and joyous reunions she had imagined, her friends listened to her story and consoled her. They never met Anthony but sensed he had become a significant part of Rebecca's life, and thought to themselves he may have been 'the one.' Her girlfriend from Pennsylvania suggested Rebecca reignite the relationship with Anthony after he graduated. But it was too much to hope for. They had dated for three months, not long enough to consider waiting for three years. She was certain they would go their separate ways and prayed they would both find someone to share their lives with. Her friends gave her the support she needed, but it didn't lessen the heartache she felt every waking hour.

She finally arrived at her parents' house. They were so happy to have her home they didn't realize how depressed she was. Rebecca was no longer used to her mother's frequent suggestions or her father's obsession with barbershop music. She loved them but realized she could live with them only until she could find a job and a place to live.

She felt at home in rural New Jersey. There were nearby mountains and lakes, and the ocean was only a few hours away. The state offered four distinct seasons, and she never tired of the beautiful landscape around her parents' home. Being away for eight years made her realize how special it was. She allowed herself time to relax and enjoy the outdoors, but her principal task was to prepare for her dental boards. Taking them at an unfamiliar school was a disadvantage, and she had to scramble to find patients she could use for the boards. A friend of the family was a dentist, and he allowed Rebecca to screen her friends and relatives at his office, and even found a patient for her.

Rebecca was jittery taking the board, and in the end, she did not pass because she did not finish. She had problems with lab work, and a distorted casting on her gold inlay meant she could not cement it on the day of the boards. She had to wait several months before another dental board exam was offered. In the meantime, all the new dentists who passed the boards were interviewing for jobs. Her struggles at dental school strengthened her resolve, and she found temporary work while she waited for her career to begin.

A bright spot was the new friend she made, who had recently moved to the area. Rebecca met Maureen at the insurance company where they worked. The girls became fast friends since they were new to the area and were the same age. They enjoyed walking around the company's park-like complex and went out clubbing on Friday and Saturday nights. Maureen had friends in the area, so because of her, Rebecca's social life was not a complete loss.

***

Anthony kept busy that summer and adhered to a predictable routine. On Monday nights, Mrs. Capalini had him over for dinner. Anthony was her only summer tenant. Sometimes when she saw him outside, Mrs. Capalini asked him to come in for tea. He didn't want hot tea in the summer, but he always accepted with a smile. He drove to the lake, sailed, and dined with Aunt Sophie and Uncle Mark. On Thursday, Friday, and Saturday nights, he worked as a bartender for Chuck and helped with accounting and inventory. He even took care of Ralphie when needed. At 7 pm on Sunday, he went to Mass and spent many hours painting and repairing the apartment.

The first trip to the Hinky Dinky with his landlady was an adventure. They drove in Anthony's big old Cadillac, which had plenty of room in the trunk for groceries. He brought her on a Monday since he had the day off and planned to have dinner with her that night. When they arrived at the Hinky Dinky, Mrs. Capalini jumped out and dashed towards the shopping carts. He followed and thought this trip might be quicker than he imagined. He shopped more carefully now that he had time to cook, and the delicious meals Mrs. Capalini prepared for him on Monday nights inspired him as he tried to cook for himself. His favorite was eggplant Parmesan, and after a few abject failures, he figured out how to prepare it. Of course, the sauce was not from scratch like Mrs. Capalini's, but the result was still tasty and something he could serve guests.

He was filling his cart with fresh fruits and vegetables when Mrs. Capalini approached him. She was upset and speaking Italian.

"My cart is stolen!" she gasped.

Anthony's adrenaline kicked in. "Do they have your purse?"

"No, it's right here. We should call the police."

"Let me find the store manager," he said softly to calm her down.

He tracked down the store manager, who looked amused. "Is this your first time shopping with this lady?"

"Well, yes, why do you ask?"

"Because she is a regular customer who has reported her cart stolen several times. I suggest you look for it in the frozen food section." Then the guy winked at him.

"Mrs. Capalini, the manager said to look for a cart in the frozen food section. It could be yours." They walked to the back of the store.

"That's it," she said in triumph.

Anthony wondered why Rebecca hadn't mentioned this issue to him. It would have helped if he had been prepared, but perhaps she didn't think he would bring the landlady to the grocery store.

***

Anthony was becoming a skilled bartender. He was friendly and laid-back and tried to diffuse trouble before it happened. Most patrons appreciated his demeanor, and he became a fixture at the jazz club. He didn't, however, expect to be called to the microphone and suspected Chuck was behind the Saturday night ritual. Around midnight, the regulars started chanting "Tony ... Tony " and continued until he left the bar and joined the musicians on stage. The local musicians knew the arrangements he was familiar with, and after a time he became more comfortable singing in front of a crowd and started to enjoy it. His performance brought many interested females to the bar afterward, and he was always polite but aloof. They were looking for a rock star, not an overworked dental student. Although he sorely missed being with a woman, he would never be with a girl just for a night; besides, he was still pining for Rebecca.

He had an open invitation from Aunt Sophie and Uncle Mark to visit the lake. Whenever he was on the water, he thought about Rebecca and the image of her on the lake during the golden hour when they sailed back to the marina. He missed her more than he thought possible. His aunt and uncle knew he hurt and supported him; they were superb listeners and encouraged him to talk about her. Uncle Mark saw something special in Rebecca and could understand Anthony's sense of loss.

Anthony hated to admit he had returned to his old dull self. He didn't drink or smoke; there were no women, and he adhered to a weekly routine. Only one pleasure remained — the library. He could still get lost in a romance novel. His favorites were historical romance novels where the hero, who shunned polite society, had confidence in himself regardless of what others thought. His female love interest was also unconventional and left on the shelf. Both had a desire to avoid the conventions of society and found happiness and fulfillment with each other. Anthony yearned for his happy ending, and the stories gave him hope. He was certain the young librarian noticed his choices; they both blushed when he checked out one with an especially steamy cover. Anthony gained insight into the female mind and tried to understand them. He realized his affair with Rebecca had a beginning and an end, and was planned. Life was rarely that straightforward. They found extraordinary passion, urgency, and desperation because they were on the clock. Their affair was dramatic. In his wildest dreams, he never imagined himself in the passionate journey of the roller coaster romance they had experienced. He wouldn't trade those days for anything. He knew circumstances had driven them during those crazy three months, and the degree of intensity was unsustainable. But when he dreamed of Rebecca, it was of times they shared doing everyday things as a couple, and he was hoping to share a lifetime of ordinary days with her. But as time passed, it felt more unlikely that this would happen. Professional schools offered a soul-crushing regimen that left the students with little energy to work on romance. How he had managed those three incredible months with Rebecca he couldn't say; in hindsight, she made the right decision when she left, but that didn't make his heart ache any less.

Chapter 33

Anthony convinced Mrs. Capalini to discontinue the lawn service and buy a lawnmower. She was not well off; she was a widow on social security, and her only additional income was from the rental properties. Her generosity to the students was reflected in the rent, which was very reasonable. She didn't make a big profit on the apartments. He was happy to mow the lawn for her and expected to do it for the next three years. As he put gas in the mower, he noticed Ellen's car; she had already moved out, but he assumed she still had things to pack. When he finished mowing, he saw her sitting on her landing.

"Ellen, hi. I didn't know you were outside."

"It's been like watching a pool boy," she joked.

"Very funny. Can I help you with anything?"

"There are just a few items to move, but sure."

He walked into an empty apartment that was partially furnished. Ellen handed him a box of dishes. "I hear there will be two female dental students moving in."

"That's right. Mrs. Capalini wanted to rent it out to women, so I told Mrs. Susman there was a nice two-bedroom close to the dental school. She placed the two incoming freshmen."

"I have enjoyed my four years living here with Donna but am ready for a place of my own. She was a wonderful roommate, but the apartment is small, and we had limited storage space. Chuck is unhappy with my move, but I will only be 45 minutes away, and it is close to my residency."

Anthony frowned. The truth is, Chuck had been moping around for weeks.

Ellen sighed. "I miss Rebecca, Anthony."

"I miss her too."

"I am worried about you, Anthony. I know how hard it was for you to let go of that relationship; it is lonely during the summer without your class here. I am a good listener if you want to talk."

Ellen hesitated to discuss her personal life but then realized if she did not have Rebecca to talk to, Anthony might be the next best person. She had concerns about Chuck and needed Anthony not as Chuck's roommate or Rebecca's boyfriend but as her friend ready to listen and someone who knew Chuck better than she did.

"I'm not sure I should start a serious relationship with Chuck. I am hesitant because he seems overprotective and sometimes even jealous."

"Aren't you already involved?"

"Not like you think. Chuck and I have been spending time together, mostly as friends."

Anthony was surprised but didn't think this was any of his business. But then he realized Ellen had the wrong impression, and he wanted his two friends to have a chance at a relationship like the one he had with Rebecca. He realized he needed to step in.

"Of course, Ellen, I have no idea what it's like being a girl dating Chuck, but I understand his feelings and insecurities. Chuck isn't the possessive type, but he is anxious about dating you. He's worried you will want someone better than him, and wonders if what you want is another doctor. Your profession and your accomplishments are so impressive he feels inadequate. He admires you and wonders if you will ever accept an ordinary guy like himself."

"That's ridiculous. Chuck is a successful businessman, has more friends than anyone I know, and is funny and kind ... "

He smiled. Ellen's defense proved that she had strong feelings for Chuck.

" I spend most of my free time with him, and our relationship has been exclusive. How can I help Chuck get past this?"

"All I know is my insecurities about Rebecca diminished when I knew she wanted to be with me. Emotional barriers lifted when we were able to relax and enjoy each other. She boosted my ego, which had been in the tank for many years. That made all the difference in the world to both of us. Even though she moved on, she left me in a better place."

***

Ellen thought about what Anthony had said and realized she didn't want Chuck to be insecure about her intentions. That night, Chuck traveled to Ellen's apartment to help her move furniture. There were boxes everywhere, and the bed that had just been delivered needed to be assembled. The apartment was hot because the air conditioning was not working. Ellen watched him struggle with the assembly and felt embarrassed as he helped her with the mattress.

"Can I get you a beer?" she asked.

"Sure, Ellen."

She took a long look at him as he rested. He wasn't handsome, but he was cute; he had a boyish smile, and his blue eyes sparkled when he joked around. His brown hair was messy and fell forward on his forehead, and he hadn't shaved that day. He was tall and big, with strong arms and a powerful physique. He sometimes didn't have the social finesse of her medical colleagues, but he was funny and likable and never meant to offend anyone. The way he looked at her made her uncomfortable; he adored her. She didn't understand him, though she never encouraged him; he was hopelessly drawn to her. She felt she didn't deserve the attention, and up to this point, she hadn't reciprocated. Ellen knew that if they took the step towards intimacy, it would be a commitment, and she shouldn't allow it to happen unless she was serious about him. She had not looked to Chuck as a potential soulmate, but being with him was starting to feel right. As he sat on the bed, overheated, tired, and doing everything she asked, she experienced overwhelming tenderness towards him that surprised her. She remembered what Anthony had said — that she hadn't taken him as seriously as she should have. She gave him the beer and sat next to him.

"Thank you for helping me with the furniture."

"You're welcome."

She gave him a sultry look. "I'm very appreciative, Chuck."

"You are?"

"Yes, I'd like to show you how much I appreciate you."

"Really?"

She took his beer and placed it on the nightstand. She gave him a scorching kiss and slid her palms underneath his shirt and onto his chest.

Chuck was overcome with desire. He tried to calm himself, after all, this was Ellen, his good friend and the person he most enjoyed being with. They had been a couple for months, but this was the first time she had encouraged him to touch her. There was no way he could misinterpret her intent; Ellen was all woman, worldly and sensual, and probably longing for a man just as much as he was craving a woman. He could burst into flames at any moment. As he unbuttoned her blouse, she revealed herself to him, and she was more lovely than he had ever imagined. Chuck was captured by her voluptuous beauty and the dizzying reality that she was ready to give herself to him.

Ellen had never seen him without his shirt. The only time she had seen abs like that was on a calendar, and she admired his sexy physique. Suddenly, she wanted him more than anything. He was a man of great passion, fearless yet sensitive, powerful, and desirable. Chuck made her feel sexy and beautiful as he told her how gorgeous she was, and Ellen couldn't get over the intense magnetism she felt for him; he was an amazing lover. He instinctively knew how to make her feel aroused, but if hesitant about what she wanted him to do, he would ask in the most explicit but polite way. He teased her, made her laugh, and made her blush, and asked her to say things she never said out loud. It was erotic, it was funny, and it was incredibly satisfying being with Chuck. She started out feeling obligated to him and ended up begging for him, and he wouldn't settle for anything less than mutual surrender to intimacy. He kissed her passionately afterward. But then Chuck, being Chuck, had to talk about it.

"Ellen, thank you. That was amazing. You're amazing. I didn't realize my maintenance skills were so important to you."

"You seem to have other skills important to me, Chuck."

"Do you have any other furniture that needs to be assembled?"

She smiled.

"I knew it would be like that, you being a doctor and all."

Ellen put her face against his chest to stifle her smile; the comment was ridiculous. Did he think that being a doctor gave her some special skills? The truth is, it was all Chuck. She was just a willing participant, as he was the one who made the experience glorious.

Chuck feasted his eyes on Ellen. She was so beautiful. She had a full figure that most women would flaunt, but she always hid behind her business-like attire. He looked at her longingly. "Now I know why you're so modest, Ellen. You don't want to distract all the male doctors and patients."

She pretended to be insulted but smiled at him. "Are my outfits too conservative for you, Chuck?"

"Oh, no. I like the way you dress. But I would like to see you in sexy outfits, when we're alone, that is."

"Should I go to the mall?"

"No, Ellen," he whispered. "Let me take care of it."

Ellen once again tried to hide her smile. The thought of Chuck in the lingerie department amused her, and she was sure he would choose some outrageous undergarments that she normally wouldn't think to wear. He made her feel sexy enough to wear anything. Sex was fun and satisfying with Chuck, and she wondered why she had waited so long to give him the attention he needed.

Chuck couldn't stop smiling. He knew they were well-suited; she just had to give it a chance. And that was a turning point, the start of a rewarding relationship that would only strengthen with time.

Chapter 34

When Anthony met him at the airport, Pinkish was happy, relaxed, and ready for sophomore year. He described his summer and talked about Ira and the things they did together. Pinkish seemed content to continue his long-distance relationship with Ira until the timing was right for marriage. Anthony didn't know how strict their culture was about chaperoning engaged couples, and though he was curious about their love life, he would never ask.

Anthony was proud of his work on the apartment. It took all summer to bring it to its current state: bright, new, and roomy. Mrs. Grilli had stocked the kitchen with dishes and cooking essentials, and Anthony donated the items they wouldn't need to avoid clutter. Pinkish was eager to prepare Indian dishes for his new roommate. This was so much nicer than the cramped quarters Pinkish had tolerated freshman year. When Anthony woke up in the morning, Pinkish had coffee brewing and sat in the living room with a book in his hands.

"What is this?" he asked.

Anthony looked at the steamy cover and blushed. "You didn't see that, Pinkish."

"What do you mean I don't see it? It is sitting right here in my hands!"

"It is an expression, 'you didn't see this'. It means even though you did see it, you need to act like you didn't see it."

Pinkish threw his hands up in the air. "You guys are so confusing! I am thinking I will never be able to understand all of this."

"Listen, Pinkish, the other guys in the class would make fun of me if they knew I was reading romance novels. And good roommates keep secrets for each other."

"I understand," said Pinkish after a pause. Then he gave him a hopeful look. "Can I read it when you finish?"

"Sure, Pinkish."

Anthony groaned. He was sure Pinkish would have questions about the book. There was a language issue, a cultural issue, and since it was a historical romance, Pinkish would have to remember the setting was England in the 1800s. Anthony's upbringing was conservative, and talking about intimate subjects felt awkward. Even when he had discussions with Rebecca, it was often in code since he was reluctant to discuss sex with her. The vision of having graphic discussions with Pinkish was mortifying, but he couldn't ask anyone else to help, or they would have to know about the romance novels.

The roommates spent the weeks before classes reading over the sophomore notes from Rebecca, and they started the year better prepared. Rebecca's classmate wrote the notes and shared them with her. The subjects were specific to dentistry: endodontics, periodontics, orthodontics, pedodontics, crown and bridge, removable dentures, and operative dentistry. And of course, dental materials. Sophomore year concentrated on lab work. The students used a high-speed dental handpiece and practiced on extracted teeth set up in stone blocks. In addition, the students practiced on plastic teeth, which required a very light touch, or the plastic would get scorched. Anthony assumed this was so that the students would not become heavy-handed. Anthony's class set up denture teeth in wax and cast inlays and crowns. Even though the second year of dental school was supposed to be the hardest, Anthony felt like he was making actual progress toward becoming a dentist.

Because he couldn't help himself, he finally wrote to Rebecca at the beginning of the school year. The letter was friendly; he wrote about the apartment, the sophomore labs, and fun stories about Pinkish and Chuck. She wrote back and told him she hadn't passed her dental boards. He wished he could have been there for her, yet he couldn't tell her that because if he exposed his true feelings, she might think it unwise to write back. He couldn't say he missed or loved her, because she would assume he was hanging on, and she didn't want that. Anthony had to remain upbeat and friendly. They had become very close friends, and it seemed reasonable for them to correspond occasionally.

***

Pinkish started bartending at Chuck's place on Friday and Saturday nights. He was a dependable employee, but sometimes the patrons teased him, which left him confused. One night, three girls were giggling as they had a conversation with Pinkish.

"No, really, I am fine," insisted Pinkish. That led to even more laughter before the girls left with their drinks. Pinkish complained to Anthony. "Those women are silly."

"What makes you say that?"

"Well, one lady kept telling me I was hot, and I kept telling her I was not."

Anthony tried to hold back a big grin. "Hot is a slang term; it means attractive, desirable, sexy."

"Really?" said Pinkish with a surprised look.

"From now on, if a girl says something you don't understand, just ask me. They like you, Pinkish, and enjoy teasing you."

Anthony had become a skilled bartender. Women who had too much to drink approached him and revealed things he should not have heard. He learned how to accept inappropriate comments without surprise or embarrassment and walked women back when they crossed the line with him without making them feel bad about themselves. Anthony tried to make the female patrons feel attractive without giving them the impression he was coming on to them. He sometimes envied Pinkish because his engagement to Ira was common knowledge, and he could always make believe he didn't understand intent if put in an awkward situation. But Anthony had no such excuse; it was evident to everyone that he was single. It amazed him to learn that women were taken by his looks, and he heard comments about his "sexy smile". He could understand why Chuck wanted to pass on the bartending duties; as a job, it was exciting and good for a guy's ego, but exhausting and caused complications if the bartender was in a relationship. Although teased constantly, Pinkish was a good sport and popular with the regulars. The atmosphere at the bar was welcoming, and the patrons rarely caused trouble. It became a social outlet and a job for both guys, and Chuck appreciated having two smart, reliable bartenders with great personalities. Anthony and Pinkish enjoyed experiences that dental school couldn't offer them: a chance to meet people and practice skills necessary to make them feel welcomed and comfortable.

***

Anthony continued to attend 7 pm Mass on Sundays. He felt a sense of peace when he went to church and enjoyed the gospel sound of the three women cantors. The music director, who played the piano, accompanied the girls. One week the girls sang without accompaniment, and they still sounded fabulous. When the Mass ended, Anthony felt a light touch on his sleeve and turned to face the music director, whose arm was in a sling.

"Hello, I'm Cathy Rycharski, the music director at the church. I couldn't help but notice the extraordinary baritone voice you have. Are you professionally trained?"

"Oh, no," he replied, " only recently I have been told I have a good voice."

"Well, our three cantors are nursing students. They noticed your voice weeks ago and wondered if you would like to join them at the 7 pm Mass."

"That's very flattering," he countered, "but surely they don't need me. They sound marvelous."

"There are arrangements they want to do, but they need a male voice. They are all in their sophomore year of nursing and are extremely busy, so we practice before the 7 pm Mass. We meet downstairs in the gathering room at 5 pm, have a light dinner together, then practice until 6:45. Please don't feel pressured, but we would love to have you join us. We will be there next Sunday at 5 pm, though I expect to be in this sling for at least two weeks."

"What happened?"

"I sprained my wrist doing something stupid. It never pays to do things in a rush."

"Thank you for the opportunity. I will think about it. I am in dental school and working and have a busy schedule too."

"It's not easy being young," observed Mrs. Rycharski. "Regardless, we're happy you attend our Mass each week. Have a great day, and once again, we do admire your talent. "

Anthony had a spiritual awakening the night he first attended church with Rebecca. After that inspirational experience, he decided to say yes to God. The invitation from the music director was a request he should agree to. But if in front of the congregation, he should receive Communion. That meant he needed to go to confession, and he would have to talk about uncomfortable subjects, like having sex before marriage, and this time it would be with a priest. Father Andrew had certainly heard it all before; after all, the congregation was mostly students. Anthony would have to admit his steamy premarital relations with Rebecca. He wondered, was it wrong to confess something he wasn't sorry for? He would have to ask.

He met with the three nursing students at 5 pm the following Sunday — Annette, Rosalind, and Martha. They gushed over him and were so happy to have him there. He was familiar with all the hymns they had planned for the service, and they were right; the addition of his voice enhanced their overall sound. Anthony had a full life, with school and work, his friendships with Pinkish, Chuck, and Joe Reilly, and his responsibilities helping Mrs. Capalini and Ralphie. But he found his favorite part of the week was 5 pm on Sunday.

Chapter 35

Halloween approached, and Anthony recalled the bizarre series of events that led to the encounter with Rebecca on the porch. Those circumstances were surprising; he hadn't planned to attend the party or go as a pirate, and he did not think for a moment that the girl of his dreams would be there, dressed as a mermaid. He bought a Halloween card with a cartoon showing a group of kids trick or treating, one dressed as a pirate, and a little girl dressed as a mermaid. The mermaid had red hair. He sent the card, hoping it would stir up happy memories from a year ago. The jazz club had its big party on Halloween night, a Friday. Pinkish was Superman, and Anthony didn't care what he was, so Chuck gave him the Zorro costume from last year. Chuck begged Ellen to come as Raggedy Ann since he never had the chance to talk to her the night of the medical school party. He dressed as Raggedy Andy and looked ridiculous. He was determined to win Ellen's heart, but Anthony suspected Chuck already had it since Ellen thought her big, funny, overenthusiastic boyfriend was adorable.

Rebecca wrote back to let him know she was waiting for her New Jersey license to be issued after a successful board exam. He was happy for her but worried the struggle was ongoing. Rebecca had no dental connections in New Jersey and would choose from the jobs the other recent graduates were unwilling to take.

***

At dental school, they were no longer seated alphabetically, and Anthony sat in the second row next to Amy. She was always asking him for help, not just when they were sitting next to each other in lab, but also when they frequented the health sciences library. Anthony liked to relax in his favorite beanbag chair, and one time they squished together in that chair as she sat right next to him. He was attracted to Amy but never entertained the thought of doing anything about it. He tried to be friendly and polite while keeping his distance. Sometimes, he thought she was flirting with him, but always concluded he was just a convenient source of information. But he had the wrong impression. He realized it while visiting his parents over the Christmas break. Anthony was at a bar with two of his high school buddies. They lived in a small town, and Anthony met his friends at the local pub. Amy was there with another girl from their class.

"Look, there's the prom queen and the head cheerleader," said Anthony's friend.

Anthony had a bored expression. "I see Amy all the time. She sits next to me in dental school."

"Has she changed?" asked his other friend.

"No."

Just then, Amy walked over to their table. She ignored his nerdy friends and went right to Anthony.

"How was your Christmas?" she asked.

"Very nice. And yours?"

"Good. Are you busy, Anthony? There is something I would like to discuss with you. Would you like to take a walk with me?"

Anthony shrugged. "Okay."

When they strolled outside, she led him down a path lined with white Christmas lights. Then she stopped. "Anthony, I get the feeling you have been avoiding me. I want to be friends again, like when we were kids."

"We are Amy."

"Really?"

"Well, we grew up together and are both in dental school. That counts for something."

She was hovering very close to him. He could see his breath, but he didn't feel cold. She smiled, put her arms around him, and kissed him deeply and deliberately. He shuddered, not because he disliked her attention, but because she stirred feelings that he had tried to suppress. She felt his hesitation and then turned up the heat. He kissed her back with a passion and a hunger that surprised them both. As she leaned into him, his response pleased her, and she wanted more. For a few minutes, he lost his composure and gave in to the temptation. Then he stepped back. Though he had thoughts of her lying on his bed, he knew Amy was not right for him, and he resisted. What if they got involved, and he ended up with her? The scenario cooled him.

"I'm sorry, this isn't a good idea," he said softly.

"Are you kidding?" was her startled response." Are you going to kiss me like that and walk away?"

"I'm sorry," he said. "You're desirable and attractive, but we have been down this road before."

"Are you still mad about prom? We were just kids. I have grown up since then, and I have changed."

"That may be true, but I have changed too. You need to find someone else, Amy."

"Anthony, you don't kiss someone like that if you don't have feelings for them. Why not try? It's obvious you want me."

Anthony took a deep breath. He didn't trust his male hormones. He had imagined what it would be like to have her, and his awkward response was brutally honest.

"You see, Amy, I have a pretty clear idea of what I want, and you're not it."

His response was like a slap in the face that she never expected. Amy was not used to rejection. The look she gave him should have killed him, but without a word, she turned and stormed down the path.

He needed a few minutes to regain his composure. When he returned to his friends, they gave him a questioning look.

"We thought you took off with the prom queen."

"Oh, no ... we just talked about school."

"Really? Then why do you have lipstick on your neck?"

Anthony groaned. No matter how hard he tried, he couldn't keep his personal life to himself. "Oh, that," he said. "She was just lonely. She'll get over it."

He felt like a jerk after he said it. Amy had been honest, and he didn't want to hurt her. He should have realized she had been seeking his attention ever since they started dental school. They grew up together, and because they both had older brothers who were involved in Little League, football, and Boy Scouts, their families were always attending the same functions. They were told to play together when their older brothers were busy with activities, and became close friends. Amy matured and began getting the attention of older boys by the time she reached middle school. She was quite beautiful and became very popular. Anthony dreamed of dating her, but he was far less experienced than the boys she was used to. He thought he had caught up with her when she hinted she needed a prom date. When she dropped him, he was devastated, and as the years went by, Anthony avoided her. The basic friendship was still there, waiting to be rediscovered, and he was still hopelessly attracted to her. If the prom incident had not happened, he could see them ending up together; she was no longer the prom queen but a serious student who would be a doctor in a few years. Of course, she had changed; he had too. But then Anthony thought of 17-year-old Rebecca being polite and kissing her prom date to avoid hurting his feelings. She was far more sensitive than Amy; she never would have tossed him aside right before prom. The enormous obstacle to Amy or any other girl was Rebecca because Anthony was still in love with her.

Anthony stayed at the bar and had another beer with his friends, but left soon afterwards. Amy drove home after her rendezvous with Anthony. He was upset that the encounter ended with an abrupt departure.

Rebecca wrote to Anthony after Christmas. She tried to be upbeat but sounded lonely. Even though he was not dating Rebecca, Anthony felt guilty about kissing Amy and could not justify his behavior. He understood how easily a guy could surrender to a seduction and then face trouble. His discipline and restraint wavered because he still had feelings for Amy and was lonely too. When he returned to school, Amy wouldn't talk to him or even look at him. He assumed he could expect this treatment for the rest of the semester.

***

Joe Reilly lived in the upstairs apartment and sometimes spent evenings with Anthony and Pinkish. They watched football, and Pinkish would cook Indian food for Joe and Anthony. Joe had a steady girlfriend, and the other guys worked, so they didn't get together often. When Joe announced he was getting married on the weekend before spring break, Anthony thought it sudden, but not surprising. Joe's girlfriend was already staying with Joe most of the time.

The wedding would take place at St. Michael's church and Joe asked Anthony, Annette, Martha, and Rosalind to sing at the ceremony. The couple couldn't find a reception hall on short notice, so Chuck offered the jazz club for the afternoon and early evening. Even though the reception would end at nine, the guests were welcome to stay at the club if they wanted an afterparty. Joe invited the entire class, and all of his friends changed their spring break plans to attend the wedding.

Joe's brother and two of Joe's college friends took him out to local bars for his bachelor party. They had fun joking around and playing pool, and they were all drinking beer and ordering shots. Anthony and Joe's brother stayed sober because they offered to be designated drivers. They partied until the bars closed, then Anthony drove Ron and Roy home before he traveled back to the house with Joe and Pinkish. They were a few blocks away when Joe started to cry.

"Are you sick?" asked Pinkish.

But Joe put his face in his hands; he was embarrassed. Anthony parked the car.

"Pinkish, I'm going to bring Joe up to his apartment. You look like you need to crash."

Pinkish looked confused. "I think I'd rather find my bed."

When Anthony and Joe were alone in the upstairs apartment, Joe started talking. "Tony, I'm not ready for all of this."

"You're just having second thoughts. Do you love her?"

"I think so, but I need more time to be sure."

"Well, postpone the wedding. Take your time and enjoy a longer engagement."

"We can't."

Anthony suspected all along but didn't want to assume. Joe was facing a life-changing challenge that would be very difficult.

"She's pregnant. I don't know how this happened," Joe sobbed. "We thought we were careful."

Anthony had met Joe's girlfriend several times, and didn't think Joe was making a mistake.

"Listen, Joe, the worst years of dental school are past us. Pinkish and I are here to help you out, and Mrs. Capalini will too. Think of how thrilled she will be to have a baby next door; she will be like a surrogate grandmother. Maybe the baby will even learn Italian!"

He had Joe smiling at the thought. Joe had no Italian in his background.

"I believe everything happens for a reason. Talk to Father Andrew; he's like a saint, and won't judge you. You are doing the right thing. It will work out, Joe."

Anthony helped Joe take off his shoes and led him to the bedroom. Joe passed out as soon as his head hit the pillow. Anthony looked around at the room he had spent so much time in. Rebecca's room. The pretty spring quilt was no longer on the bed, but everything else looked the same. The heartache became overwhelming once again. It had been a year since he had stayed in this room caring for Rebecca after her wisdom tooth surgery. He ignored his feelings by keeping busy, but now the memories haunted him. Anthony took a few minutes to compose himself as he sat in Joe's living room. He remembered all the time he spent here with Rebecca, and how they made love in every room. She brought out the very best in him and taught him to love. He lingered in the apartment for several more minutes as he tried to pull himself together; he didn't want Pinkish to see him cry.

***

The wedding was the social event of the year, and the bride and groom looked happy and content. Anthony was sure the girls in the class would notice the loose-fitting wedding dress and the small baby bump, but nobody judged them, and everyone wished them the best. The music at the ceremony was phenomenal. Martha sang *'We've Only Just Begun'* with such emotion that there wasn't a dry eye in the church. Jazz musicians played at the reception, and Anthony was called upon to sing *'Ain't No Sunshine'* with such haunting sadness that everyone knew he was thinking about the red-haired girl from a year ago. They were all drinking and having fun when Amy approached Anthony and asked him to dance. It was a slow number, so they could talk.

"Anthony, I owe you an apology. I put you in an awkward situation when I knew we would have to sit next to each other for the rest of the year."

"Are you calling a truce?"

"I believe I am."

He looked into Amy's big blue eyes. She was beautiful.

Amy sighed. "I believed we had a connection because we grew up together. I hoped we could try to have an adult relationship."

"Oh, Amy," he whispered, "when I was 17 years old, I was more than willing. I was an awkward teenage boy but was quite sensitive, and I would have learned how to make things exciting for you. I would have done anything you wanted."

"You're killing me with your words, Anthony."

They danced in silence for a minute or two. Then, she gazed into his eyes. "You're still in love with Rebecca, aren't you?"

"I'm afraid so."

"Well, that explains everything." She smiled. "Let me know if you change your mind. I have feelings for you and would like to give it a second chance. I have changed, you know."

"I believe you have Amy. And I also have feelings for you. We have a history."

"We do. Perhaps we should have kept it a friendship all along."

"Maybe. But friendship is always a good place to start."

Chapter 36

The sophomores prepared to work on the clinic floor after spring break. They practiced their skills in the lab for most of the year, and now they were ready to practice on each other. The first activity was rubber dam placement. In the clinic, the students did their operative dentistry with a rubber dam placed on the patient to achieve a clear field and to prevent the patient from swallowing or aspirating small objects. Pinkish was Anthony's partner, and they placed the rubber dam on each other. The clamp was a little uncomfortable without anesthesia, but Anthony and Pinkish got the hang of it. They practiced taking X-rays on a dummy named Dexter, but the process was easier on a subject who wasn't plastic, so they took a full series of X-rays on each other without difficulty. The next step was to take alginate impressions. Sometimes it took five or six tries before they got an acceptable result. When they practiced injections, one day the entire sophomore class was numb on the upper left; the next day the lip and tongue were all numb on the lower right. Giving the injection was worse than getting it. Anthony's hand was trembling when he approached Pinkish. They both started laughing because of nerves.

"Do not be afraid," Pinkish said as he waggled his eyebrows, "I am honored to be your first."

They both started laughing so hard that they had trouble regaining their composure. They didn't want to draw attention to themselves, so Anthony administered the lidocaine. Pinkish assured him it didn't hurt at all. Anthony knew he was lying.

The school somehow found sixty-seven people who needed a one-surface amalgam to be the first procedure done on a person. The students had become incredible actors because they were more apprehensive than the patients. Anthony's first patient was a sixteen-year-old who was not worried at all. Anthony gave him a mandibular block injection and was relieved when the anesthesia was profound on the lip and tongue. The instructor checked for adequate anesthesia. Anthony put the rubber dam on the patient. The instructor checked it. He prepared the tooth for an ideal retention form. The instructor checked it. He removed the decay. The instructor checked. He filled the tooth and adjusted the occlusion. The instructor checked. An hour and fifteen minutes later, the kid had the most beautiful amalgam on tooth #30. The patient's father was waiting for him.

"How many did you have filled?" he asked his son.

"One."

Anthony was sorry the simple procedure took so long, but when he reflected on the experience, he considered it a breakthrough. The patient's filling would last a long time. The father paid a reduced fee. Although the boy had to sit for an hour and fifteen minutes, Anthony knew he didn't hurt him. Overall, the day was a success.

***

Rebecca called Ellen late one night. Phone calls were expensive, and long-distance calls were less costly after 10 pm. They exchanged letters but had not spoken to each other since the summer.

"Hi Ellen, I miss you. I wish I could walk next door and have coffee with you."

"I know how you feel. Those were hard times, but I sometimes miss those days."

"How's your residency and how is Chuck?"

" Good. Chuck already proposed to me; you know he is so anxious."

"Really? Ellen, I think he's afraid he might lose you. What did you say?"

"I told him I don't believe in long engagements and that I am not ready to get married."

"Ellen, you know he will eventually wear you down."

"I know. But I am busy with residency, and I have such a grueling schedule. I am amazed that we have so much fun despite crazy and conflicting commitments. An engagement would add another layer of pressure. Why change when everything is just fine? I am happy with the way things are now. What's new with you, Rebecca?"

" Well, I didn't want to write it in a letter, but I met someone. Remember when I told you about the local ADA meeting? I am the only woman in the chapter and look like somebody's daughter instead of a colleague. Most of the dentists are my dad's age. But there is one young dentist two years older than me, and after the second time meeting him, he asked me out."

"So tell me about him."

"His name is Patrick; he's Irish Catholic, and my mother is hopeful because he checks off all the boxes. He's already well established, and he's a nice guy."

"How about your boxes, Rebecca? Does he check all of them?"

"Well, that's why I want your advice. Remember three questions: do you trust him, does he make you feel safe and does he take your breath away?"

"I remember."

" There's a problem with the last one."

"Why Rebecca?"

"I don't know."

After a long pause on the phone, Rebecca explained. "We haven't had physical contact, but I'm not feeling it."

"It's hard to settle when you've had it all."

"It is."

" I can't tell you what to do, Rebecca, but I can tell you about my experience. You know I was engaged. I thought he was the man of my dreams, since he checked the boxes: charming, well-off, handsome, an established businessman who knew how to say all the right things. But it didn't work out. The relationship was passionate, but without much laughter or fun. He couldn't accept the demands of my profession, and the engagement ended suddenly, and it was devastating. But then I met this crazy funny guy who didn't check any of the boxes, or so I thought. Chuck accepts my schedule and does everything he can to make my life easier. He owns a bar, which doesn't satisfy my family, but my family's lack of enthusiasm doesn't matter. He relieves the stress in my life and makes me happy. I trust him; I feel safe, and though love has grown slowly, he takes my breath away. I know this may confuse you even more, but you should follow your heart, Rebecca. That's all I can say."

"Thanks, Ellen. You have helped me more than you will ever know."

Part III

The Pursuit

JD Henning

Chapter 37

Anthony started work at the dental clinic in the spring of 1981, developed his skills, and worked confidently by the time he was a senior. Rebecca was right about his chairside manner. The patients appreciated his careful, gentle approach, and many requested him. Because he practiced all week at the clinic and worked part time at the bar, his schedule was busy, and the last semester of his dental school career came upon him quickly. As they ushered in 1983, Anthony, Pinkish, and Chuck realized the camaraderie at work would soon end. New Year's Eve was the last major holiday working together at the jazz club. Pinkish would return to India in the summer to marry Ira, and Anthony would start his dental career, still considering his plans. He had an idea of what he would like to do.

All the problem students in the back row freshman year had surprised the instructors since every single one was on schedule to graduate on time. Ron Zee still looked like he belonged in a rock band, and Roy Tanoa wore flip-flops whenever he could. Amy graduated at the top of her class. She was a dedicated dentist with an aptitude for performing root canals and would complete her training at an endodontic specialty program in Chicago. With her looks, she could have married a rich guy and had an easy life; instead, she chose to pursue her career and help others. Joe Reilly's little girl turned two. The Reillys planned to stay in town and move to the downstairs apartment when Anthony and Pinkish moved out. Anthony and Pinkish babysat many times. Anthony thought it would be years before he was changing diapers and preparing bottles, but at twenty-five, he got a taste of what it was like to be a parent. Pinkish was a big help because he was the oldest of a large family and had taken care of his younger siblings. Between the two of them, they were wonderful babysitters for one little girl who got plenty of attention. Mrs. Capalini was thrilled that the Reilly family would move into the downstairs apartment, and she felt like part of the family. The baby was always so content sitting on Mrs. Capalini's lap.

The class of 1983 realized the hard path was not over after graduation. Dentistry was stressful. Many patients were afraid, and gaining their trust proved challenging. People came in with problems you wished they didn't have, but you had to fix them. The responsibility was enormous. The focus was always on the person in the dental chair asking for your help, and the dentist's feelings and needs always took a back seat. Anthony knew the profession would always be difficult, so he planned an outlet for himself in the years to come. His dream was to be by the ocean and to sail in his free time. He contacted his cousin, who was looking for an apartment in the same seaside town Anthony visited throughout his childhood; it was a place he loved. Anthony wanted to move to New Jersey and room with his cousin. He still questioned his decision to go into dentistry. Chuck was an example of an entrepreneur who saw a need and created a successful business after college without a postgraduate degree. He owned the house he was living in and planned to rent it to professional students in the future. He had no student loans to pay, owned real estate, and made money in the years after college. Anthony was just a potential earner. It would take time to establish himself and pay off his loans. But he earned the right to be called 'doctor', which was something to be proud of. He had to go through hell to get there. He realized that one has to love the profession to make it worthwhile.

***

On a brisk Friday afternoon in January, Anthony stopped by Chuck's house as promised to walk Ralphie after finishing work at the clinic. When he opened the door, Ralphie was dancing about because Ellen was giving him a treat. Running into Ellen was a surprise.

"Hi Ellen, I just stopped by to walk Ralphie."

"Well, Anthony, I was just about to walk Ralphie."

"Perhaps we should walk together."

The day was perfect for a walk; brisk but sunny.

"I haven't seen you since before Christmas, Anthony. What's new?"

"Nothing much; I continue to work at the clinic and at the club. I am also looking into opportunities for the future."

" Do you know where you want to practice?"

"There are no job prospects yet, but I plan to move in with my cousin in New Jersey."

This was news to Ellen.

"Does Rebecca know? Have you heard from her?"

"We exchanged Christmas cards, but I didn't mention my plans to move."

They walked for a few blocks in silence. Then Ellen decided she had to get involved. "I have listened to you and Rebecca for the past three years. I appreciate that neither of you sought information from me, as I would hate to be caught in the middle. But I must ask, did your decision have anything to do with Rebecca?"

"I made the decision because I want to settle near my cousins in New Jersey and have always dreamed of living in a beach community. But Rebecca is still on my mind."

Ellen knew the time had come, as a friend to both Anthony and Rebecca, for her to intervene. She also sensed Anthony had kept his feelings hidden for a long time.

"Anthony, she is not seeing anyone. She has three jobs, but they are merely stepping stones until she finds something better. This information is my gift to you, and it's up to you what you choose to do with it."

Anthony was so quick to hug Ellen that he almost let go of Ralphie's leash. Then he pulled back. "If Chuck saw that, he would deck me first and ask questions later."

Ellen laughed. "Chuck still doesn't realize he has nothing to worry about."

"How many times has he proposed?"

"Five. But I never say no."

"You better have a medical kit the day you say yes. I'm sure he could faint."

Anthony was determined to take charge of his destiny. After finishing his requirements, he would graduate, move to New Jersey, and win back the heart of the girl he couldn't forget. He didn't know if she had feelings for him, so he would have to be subtle. He didn't want her to feel obligated or pressured.

***

Rebecca was feeling down. The winter was cold, and being single on Valentine's Day depressed her. She shared an apartment with a woman who had a steady boyfriend. Most of her colleagues at work were married. She had attended countless weddings and baby showers in the last two years and was starting to feel like the world was passing her by. But then, a surprise: two Valentine's cards in the mailbox. One was from Anthony; the other, from Ellen. She opened Anthony's card. The card featured a cute puppy that looked like Ralphie, and its note read, 'Happy Valentine's Day. Thinking of you. Love, Anthony.' Rebecca wasn't sure how much she should read into that note.

Next, she opened Ellen's card, which was funny and sexy, with a photo of a hunky guy on the cover. Inside Ellen wrote, 'My Valentine's message for you. Anthony is available.'

She felt a flash of heat. When she looked at the card, the model resembled Anthony. Ellen must have talked to him. Could this lead to something? In truth, she thought about him all the time. She wrote back to him that day and told him she was thinking about him too.

Anthony wanted to ease Rebecca back into a relationship and invited her to his graduation. He planned to send a plane ticket regardless of whether she could come. The most romantic gesture he could think of was the gift of a song. But which one? He found perfect lyrics and knew with the help of Mrs. Rycharski, Annette, Rosalind, and Martha he could make a heartfelt recording on cassette.

He headed to St. Michael's at 5 pm on Sunday. Since it was his turn to bring dinner, he carried a pizza, a bag of potato chips, and bottles of root beer. He hoped they would be open to his request. He asked them while he was serving the pizza.

"We have always planned on recording our sound, but haven't taken steps to make it happen. Our wonderful group will disband in a few months when we all graduate. I suggest we record at least one song as a keepsake and a memory of the music we have made together. I have a request with a special intention."

"Which song would you like to record, Anthony?"

"Not one of our hymns, and not a religious song. It's a song I would like to record for a girl."

The ladies had stopped eating their pizza and were on the edge of their seats.

'Here goes,' thought Anthony. *'It's time to pour my heart out.'*

"Three years ago I had a special girlfriend; one I can never forget. I want to revisit our relationship. Her very first connection to me was when she heard me singing in the hallway of the dental school, but at that point, she had not seen me or met me. She told me she was first attracted to my voice. I want to win her back, starting once again with my voice, so I found a song with lyrics that express my feelings; it's called *'Isn't It Time'* by the Babys."

"I know the song," said Martha. "It has a gospel vibe; I think we can do it."

"Is it the girl with the red hair?" asked Annette.

"You noticed us?"

"The two of you looked like you were in love when you came to Mass together. I couldn't help but notice."

"What happened?" asked Rosalind.

"She graduated and moved back to New Jersey. I secretly wished to keep her with me, but didn't want to hold her back."

Rosalind had tears in her eyes. "Anthony, you have to be the most romantic man on earth. We all love you so much. Of course, we'll help you win back your girl."

There was an unexpected group hug. Anthony thought these women must be angels. He played the recording for them and gave them each a cassette with the song. Mrs. Rycharski said she would look for sheet music, but added she could recreate the arrangement if she had to. They sang with renewed enthusiasm at Mass that evening. They would start their meetings at 4:30 to give them time to arrange the new song.

***

At the beginning of April, Rebecca received a note from Anthony with an invitation to graduation and a one-way plane ticket. He didn't reveal his intentions. The ticket was one-way, and she didn't know how long she would stay. She didn't know what to plan, but told her employers she needed to resolve a personal matter. She spoke to the administrator at the first office, who took one look at her and realized she was upset about something. The office manager suggested a three-week break since she thought Rebecca needed the time and she did not want to cancel and reschedule patients. Rebecca told her other employer she wanted three weeks. Unfortunately, the letter she wrote to Anthony never made it to his mailbox and was returned to her. Rebecca was heartbroken; he must think she didn't even care enough to send a reply. She didn't have his phone number, so she called Ellen. She sounded upset.

"Ellen, I need your help."

"Hi Rebecca," she said warily. "Is something wrong?"

"I wrote to Anthony a month ago, but they returned the letter to me. I don't have his phone number, and need to talk to him."

"He's probably at work now. What did the letter say?"

"I told him I would meet him at the airport."

"Oh, Rebecca, this explains so much. Anthony has not been himself. I'm sure he thinks you weren't planning to come."

"This is terrible. I have to let him know I'm coming. He has had so many disappointments in the past; I would hate for him to think I didn't care enough to write back."

"Calm down; I'll help you fix this. I can give you the work number, but sometimes it's so loud at the club they miss their calls. He's there until 2 am tonight. Do you want me to go talk to him?"

"Would you, Ellen? Just relay the message that I will be on the flight and meet him at the airport."

The next day, Rebecca received a cassette in the mail. She didn't have a cassette player since the newest trend was 8-track tapes. Her father played his barbershop music on a cassette player, but she didn't know if she would see him before her flight. She put the cassette in her purse.

Chapter 38

As Rebecca settled into the window seat on the plane, a nice older lady took the aisle. They greeted each other, then the woman commented about the beautiful day. She had a book in hand and seemed like a quiet traveling companion for the flight. Rebecca needed time to think and appreciated that she had traveled alone. She was nervous and wondered if she was getting her hopes too high for this reunion with Anthony. She wondered if he would still be attracted to her. Had he changed? Then she thought about the way she had ended their relationship. Did he understand, or would he have trouble forgiving her? She was unaware of how distressed she was until she felt large teardrops falling into her lap.

The lady next to her touched her sleeve. "Do you want to talk about it, dear?"

Rebecca looked up at her with brilliant, tear-streaked blue-green eyes. The woman introduced herself.

"My name is Agnes. I'm traveling to meet my second grandchild for the first time. I have three grown children and have become a skillful listener. Would you like to talk about it?"

"Hi, Agnes; Rebecca. I'm just suffering from a case of nerves. I'm traveling to meet an ex-boyfriend I haven't seen for three years, and I don't know what will happen."

"Pleased to meet you, Rebecca." She paused, then tried to bring her out. "Were you close to him?"

Rebecca looked at Agnes, who seemed sympathetic. She decided that she needed to talk.

"I was very close to him. We dated only a few months, but the relationship felt right. I was in love with him, but I graduated from school and returned to my family in New Jersey. He stayed in school for the next three years. A few months ago he contacted me and sent me a plane ticket with an invitation to his graduation."

"It sounds like it never ended for you. Do not hide your feelings from him; he has waited a long time to see you again."

Rebecca nodded in agreement. Of course, Agnes was right. She continued to explain. "He was sad when I left. I told him I was not breaking up with him, but was letting him go. I didn't think he was ready to commit, even though he wanted to. I begged him to make it easier for us, and even asked him to help me move. He just looked at me with the saddest expression, then said, said, *as you wish.*"

Agnes looked up. "Is that exactly what he said to you, *as you wish*?"

"Yes, why?"

"Do you read romance novels?"

Rebecca wondered why this seemed to be a relevant topic.

"No."

"Does he?" asked Agnes.

"I don't think so, but maybe."

"There is a famous romance novel I read about a year ago. The hero was a farmhand in love with a beautiful princess. Because of his subservient position in life, he couldn't say *'I love you,'* so he substituted it with '*as you wish.*' Did your boyfriend ever tell you he loved you?"

"No, but he said, '*As you wish.*'"

" Of course, I know nothing about your beau, but you should be bold and unafraid. If you're in love with him, you need to tell him."

"Thank you, Agnes. That's helpful advice. You remind me of my best friend, Ellen."

"And you remind me of myself when I was your age. It's difficult to be young." She squeezed Rebecca's hand. Rebecca wondered if the advice had something to do with the heartache Agnes faced when she was young and single.

When the plane landed, she said goodbye to Agnes and headed for the baggage claim area. She did not have a checked bag, only carry-on luggage, because she didn't know how long she would stay. It would have been inappropriate to bring a large suitcase.

She saw him before he saw her. He looked the same, but somehow more mature, even taller than she remembered. He didn't wear glasses. Her heart skipped a beat; he was so handsome. She wondered; would he feel the same way about her? Rebecca started to tear up.

Anthony spotted the tall, sultry redhead; she was a vision, and he was smitten again. She looked nervous and on the verge of tears. He rushed up to her, took her in his arms, and without a word kissed her. She melted into him. He held her tight as if he didn't want to let her go and whispered, "I missed you so much."

And she looked into his honest blue eyes and said, "I missed you too, Anthony."

Rebecca cried and could not stop. He shielded her from the concerned looks of the other passengers, but Agnes saw Rebecca as she collected her bag, and knew they were happy tears. She could tell from their body language that they would end up together. Agnes smiled at the thought that she had helped.

He brought her to his car, the old Cadillac. Meeting at the airport after three years was a shock. He took her hand and gazed into those beautiful blue-green eyes. "I'm so happy you're here, Rebecca. I didn't provide many details, but I hoped we could play it by ear and get reacquainted. Is there anything I can do to make you feel more comfortable, or is there someplace you'd like to go?"

"Anthony, I'm so emotional right now, I think I'd like to go to your apartment so we can talk."

"Listen, Rebecca, I'm sorry I came on so strong in the terminal. It's just that I miss you and was so happy to see you."

She looked at Anthony, then took a deep breath. She would not act evasive; he had waited for three years, and she should tell him what she wanted. "Anthony, I don't care where we go, I just need to be alone with you ... and not just to talk."

Anthony was already under her spell and needed to be sure he didn't misunderstand. "Do you want to be with me, Rebecca?"

"Yes, that is, if you want me."

Her comment filled him with heat and irrepressible desire; no games, no pretense, just a bold jump back into the relationship. Words could not describe his wants and his needs. The twenty-minute ride from the airport seemed like an eternity. He put in a cassette tape; all love songs.

"Oh wait, Anthony, I didn't have a cassette player, so I didn't hear this." She took the cassette he had sent her out of her purse.

"We'll save that one for last," he whispered.

They arrived in the familiar neighborhood, and everything looked the same. Anthony played his song for Rebecca,' *Isn't It Time.'* She listened to his incredible voice, and the lyrics, and knew he didn't need to say anything else.

"That's a romantic, unforgettable way to tell me how you feel. Do you think the time is right for us?"

"I do."

"Let's go inside."

The transformation of the Grilli's apartment amazed Rebecca. "The place doesn't look the same."

Anthony hesitated, then gave a measured response. "I had a lot of pent-up energy after you left."

"I'm sorry."

"Don't be. That was in the past. Let's look forward." He brought her bag in. "Should I put this in my room?"

"Sure. Excuse me, Anthony, I'd like to freshen up."

"You know where everything is. Pinkish is gone for the day, so we have the place to ourselves."

Anthony was sitting on his bed waiting for her. She sat down next to him. He held her hand for the longest time; he still could not believe they were together. They were desperate for each other, but hesitant because of the three years of separation.

"I'm a little nervous, Anthony."

He smiled. "Me too."

He brushed her hair back, kissed her hand, and moved to her lips, savoring every touch, every caress. They caressed timidly, gently. She relaxed, then surrendered to an irrepressible need and longing. As he unbuttoned her blouse, Rebecca was aware of the black lingerie she wore, a sign that she had hoped for this encounter. When he removed his shirt, appearing so strong, so powerful, she felt safe, loved, and he took her breath away. The rest of the experience was like a dream; it felt like love, and sex was just the vehicle they used to express it. They savored every moment and embraced the strong physical attraction that was still there, more intense than ever. Anthony could not believe how beautiful she looked, or that this enchanting red-haired goddess was in his bed. Only when they could not bear to be apart for another moment, he descended on her, and they connected in the way they most desperately needed. His kisses were so gentle yet filled with passion, and his movements, sensual and intense. Rebecca felt a wild yearning that she could not control, and her need, her desire, and their lovemaking led to complete surrender. She experienced a shattering sense of pleasure, satisfaction, and completion, and she brought him with her; both physically and emotionally spent as they succumbed to the intimacy.

After he filled her with his warmth, he stilled. He confessed his deep commitment. "You are a part of me, Rebecca. You will always be there. I love you; I always will."

Rebecca was full of regret. "I have loved you for a long time but didn't reveal it to you. I thought I was doing the right thing, letting you go."

He sighed. "We can't change what happened. Maybe waiting was right for us. But my heart can't wait another day."

She touched his cheek. "You don't have to wait any longer, Anthony."

He smiled at her. "I guess we didn't forget how to ... you know," he blushed and paused, softly adding, "I would like to continue to practice."

That night they practiced several times as they relaxed and enjoyed each other. Neither spoke of the past nor the future, because today was more wonderful than they could have imagined. Tomorrow would be graduation, family, and talk of the future, but today was theirs and they savored every moment.

Chapter 39

They set the alarm for 7 am since Anthony expected his family to arrive around 8 am. Rebecca didn't know what kind of reception she would get from Mrs. Roselli, but both women loved Anthony and wanted him to be happy. Mrs. Roselli had not forgotten the hurt in Rebecca's eyes when she spoke of leaving Anthony, and she knew Rebecca's decision had her son's interests in mind. She also suspected that Anthony had met his match, and she was comfortable with Rebecca.

Graduation was a joyous occasion. The dental class of 1983 was a wild and crazy group, and despite the odds, most of them had completed their studies. Against all rules and protocols, the dental school graduates were passing around a flask during the tedious graduation ceremony. Ever since the freshman year speech that insinuated they were a bunch of misfits, they had engaged in behavior that would live up to their reputation. They would not abandon this mindset because they had graduated. Even though they would go their separate ways, their reputation as a class lived on.

Anthony was thankful that his family had come. His parents, his sister Angela, Tommy, and his wife Julie, and Uncle Mark and Aunt Sophie celebrated his graduation. Aunt Edith could not attend, but Anthony promised to stop by her house on his way to his new apartment in New Jersey. Rebecca tried to stay in the background since this was a family day, but Anthony would not let her out of his sight. After a long ceremony, they went out for an early dinner, and the group planned to return the next day for a party at Anthony's apartment. Rebecca felt more relaxed around Anthony's family as the day progressed; they were welcoming, and it was clear that Anthony's happiness was their priority.

"How are you holding up, Rebecca?" he asked as they arrived at the apartment.

"I'm a little tired, but the day was wonderful. You have such a nice family, Anthony."

"They didn't stress you with too many questions, did they?"

"No, they're great. They probably realize we need some time; after all, you just picked me up at the airport yesterday."

Anthony had been waiting for the right moment to tell Rebecca about his plans. But Rebecca grabbed hold of the subject before he had the chance to.

"I have no actual plans, Anthony. I realize that my personal life is more important than my career, and I am open to changes."

"How about being together in New Jersey?" he asked.

She hesitated. "I don't understand."

" I hoped you would drive to New Jersey with me. I plan to live with my cousin at the shore and have registered for the regional board exam."

Rebecca embraced him with the enthusiasm of someone who had won the lottery. "I can't tell you how happy I am at this moment. When are you moving? I took off from work because I had hoped to spend some time together."

"Great! If we hurry with the move, we can vacation at the beach and sail in the bay."

She was so overwhelmed she fought back tears as she entered the apartment. Pinkish greeted them with two cold beers in hand. "Why are you crying, Rebecca?"

"Because I'm so happy."

Pinkish didn't know how to respond to this. "Ok. Maybe you should talk to Ira. She's in the kitchen."

The girls had just met, but they were already becoming friends. Ira was quiet and polite, five feet tall, with long dark hair and big brown eyes. She was a beautiful girl with a smile that must have captured the interest of her fiancée. She was perfect for Pinkish; their families had done a wonderful job with the match; truly a love match. Ira hugged Rebecca when she saw her happy tears. "What happened?" she asked.

"Anthony is going to move to New Jersey. We have plans, Ira. This is what I wanted for a long time."

"Well, have a good cry, Rebecca, and then dry your eyes because we're going to have a party tonight."

The party began when Ellen and Chuck joined the group. Three couples had planned a goodbye fling since Anthony and Pinkish were moving out in a few days. The bittersweet part of this graduation was that the three men were moving on with their lives and would miss working together and seeing each other. They would be together in India for the wedding of Pinkish and Ira and would keep in touch, but they had to give up the everyday camaraderie they had grown to depend on. Unusual circumstances threw together these unlikely friends. They helped each other achieve their career goals and supported each other as they pursued the partners they wanted to spend their lives with.

***

Ira and Rebecca spent the night at the apartment. When Rebecca woke up in the morning, she smelled coffee brewing, and Ira was sitting on the couch with a lavender paperback in her hands.

"Is this your book, Rebecca?"

Rebecca looked at the steamy cover. "No, it's not yours?"

Ira blushed. "No."

Rebecca took the book and looked at its spine. "It's a library book, so it could be Anthony's," she remarked.

"I am thinking it might be for Pinkish."

"What makes you think that, Ira?"

"Well," she hesitated, "lately he seems to know a little more of what he is doing. I was beginning to wonder if he was spending time with an American girl."

"Oh, Ira, I'm sure Pinkish has been faithful. He must be reading about sex in the book. By the way, you didn't see the book."

"What do you mean, I see it in your hands!"

"'You didn't see it' means even though you did see it, you must make believe you didn't because you weren't supposed to see it."

"You Americans can be so confusing. You are saying I should forget I saw it."

"That's right, Ira, and if you see another book like this, you need to make believe you didn't notice because these books might benefit us. They could make our men better lovers."

Ira blushed. "I understand."

Rebecca took the book and put it in Anthony's room in an obvious spot. Someone needed to take it back to the library.

Chapter 40

Anthony and Pinkish planned to have the party in their yard. The Reillys were home and joined the group. Even though Pinkish and Anthony were the hosts, Rebecca and Ira woke up early in the morning to prepare as their guys slept in; there was a little too much drinking and reminiscing the night before. Anthony planned to grill with charcoal and serve drinks from an ice chest filled with beer, wine coolers, and soda. Mrs. Capalini made her fabulous eggplant Parmesan as a side dish and homemade cannoli for dessert. After an afternoon of eating, drinking, and socializing, they planned to attend the 7 pm Mass at St. Michael's Church.

Anthony arrived at the church 30 minutes early for a short practice. For the last time, Anthony, Annette, Rosalind, and Martha would be cantors. Father Andrew was sorry to see them go; they had been a lively addition to the Sunday night Mass. College students attended this Mass because of the youthful enthusiasm the singing group brought each week. Parishioners, graduates, and their families filled the pews of the church. After rehearsal, Anthony approached Father Andrew and asked if he could make the announcements and say a few words at the end of Mass.

The music was an inspiration. The cantors knew it would be their last Mass. Their marvelous sound was the product of a three-year labor of love, and the group would remember it as an unforgettable moment in life. As Anthony stood up at the end of the service, he paused to look at all the familiar faces in the church that night. After a sad smile, he gazed at his musical colleagues with affection.

"It has been a privilege to sing at St. Michael's. Three years ago, three angelic voices miraculously transformed the Mass for me, and I was honored when they asked me to join their group. It was a rewarding religious experience to sing with them. I am grateful for their friendship and will always remember and keep them in my prayers. These three women graduated today with nursing degrees, and I am sure they will spend their lives caring for and healing others. Thank you, Father Andrew, Mrs. Rycharski, Martha, Rosalind, Annette, and St. Michael's, for being a refuge these last three years."

With a bow, he pointed to them, and the congregation responded with heartfelt applause. The Mass ended, and they sang the recessional hymn as Father Andrew and the altar boys walked down the center aisle. But the congregation did not leave. Instead, they all held up their lighters after someone dimmed the lights. Father Andrew seemed astonished that this would happen at a Catholic service.

"Is this like a concert?" Anthony asked.

"I guess so," said Mrs. Rycharski. " Let's do two songs," and added, "This will be great!"

Mrs. Rycharski started playing as Martha and the girls did their version of *'I Say A Little Prayer'*. Anthony didn't know the song was in their repertoire. Martha was glorious.

Then she whispered, "Anthony, you're up." The final song; *'Isn't It Time'*. It wasn't a hymn, but surprising, energetic and moving. The churchgoers were all on their feet. When Anthony's vocal was over,

Rebecca rushed up to the altar. They embraced. Anthony looked over at Father Andrew; he was standing in front of a stained glass window, glowing. Martha, Rosalind, and Annette were trying to finish the chorus but couldn't stop crying. Mrs. Rycharski, the consummate professional, continued on the piano. The parishioners were standing and cheering. Anthony scanned the crowd and saw the smiling faces of his family, Pinkish and Ira, Chuck and Ellen, the Reillys, and Mrs. Capalini. Everyone was glad and inspired. Rebecca was finally in his arms. This time he wouldn't let go.

And Anthony thought to himself, if he were the hero of a romance novel, this would be the perfect time to end the tale. There would never be a more breathtaking moment than this.

Deceptive Images

A SNEAK PEEK AT BOOK 2
DENTAL ROMANCE, ADVENTURE, AND FUN

The summer of 1972 was a turning point in Rosa Fletcher's life. The road trip with her high school friend, Angelica, was supposed to be a week of fun and horseback riding, but Rosa's touching memories of that summer vacation lingered and resonated into adulthood. It all began on a perfect evening in July.

The scenery in the Adirondacks was stunning. Rosa traveled with Angelica's parents, Mr. and Mrs. D'Augelli. As they neared their destination, the air was crisp and clean; the atmosphere, magical. A full moon peaked in and out of the cloud cover as they passed a myriad of lakes, and the moonlight sparkled on the calm waters. The car windows were open as they savored the fresh forest scent of pine and experienced a thrilling sense of adventure. When they arrived, they found a ranch nestled in the wilderness with a large private lake as its focal point and checked into a rustic two-bedroom cabin with a lake view. The girls opened the windows, unpacked their suitcases, and stretched out on the twin beds that were so comfortable after the long drive. They tried to temper their excitement and get some sleep. The first riding lesson was early in the morning.

Rosa and Angelica had breakfast while Mr. and Mrs. D'Augelli slept in. Angelica's parents were not early risers. Rosa, amused they chose a ranch for their vacation, thought Mrs. D'Augelli was glamorous and not the type to get on a horse. Her husband was there on the whim of his wife and daughter and would be more comfortable in the city or at a casino. He hoped to find a group of men who played cards. Even Rosa wondered what she was doing at the ranch. She liked horses, but the thought of riding one was terrifying. Rosa cringed when she remembered giving the horses sugar cubes when visiting her uncle in the country. She was certain it was bad for their teeth. She hovered behind Angelica when they arrived at the lesson while Cal, the cowboy in charge, zeroed in on the anxiety of his new pupil.

"Are you planning to ride today?" he asked quietly as he approached Rosa.

She hesitated. "I think so."

He smiled. "Don't worry, I will fix you up with Snowball, the sweetest, gentlest horse in the stable." He put her at ease by calling her "Rosie" and called Angelica "Angie". The cowboys used these nicknames for the girls the rest of the week, and had adopted descriptive Western names like Cal, Curly, Lindy, Wyatt, and Russ. The teasing and nicknames were all good-natured fun, and Rosa felt more comfortable attending the lesson. Afterward, Rosa and Angelica swam and enjoyed water sports available throughout the afternoon.

Before dinner, Angelica prepared for a night out. Rosa worried she didn't have the right clothes and suspected her friend Angelica was more interested in meeting boys than riding horses. Rosa took a walk to be by herself, overwhelmed with plans for the evening. She settled under a shade tree, opened her novel, and savored the solitude and the cool country breeze. A conversation in the barn interrupted her reverie.

"So there are a lot of single ladies in the group," said Cal, "so let's make sure they feel welcomed."

"No problem," bragged Lindy. He was a ladies' man.

"And Curly, make sure those two young girls get your attention. They're around your age."

" The shorter one is a little too bold for me, and I'd rather not encourage her," said Curly. "I think that could be trouble."

"Focus on the other one."

Rosa thought she would die; they were talking about her. She had to disappear before they realized she could hear them. She was sixteen and not yet ready for flirtations with older guys.

When they returned to the clubhouse that night, Angelica met a boy from college. Rosa towered over his friend, but he politely danced with her. She suspected he would prefer a dance partner more his height. The band played until 2 am, and the girls stayed until closing.

The next day, Rosa rode a different horse named Jack. Curley was the cowboy teaching the group. Rosa's heart did a little flip when she looked at Curly.

"Are you ready for a riding adventure?" he asked.

"I think so, but I'm not sure."

He assisted her, and as she settled in the saddle, she realized his teaching expertise was in helping beginners.

"Rosie, right?"

"Yes." She gazed at the beautiful blond curls that reached the collar of his shirt. "And you're Curly?"

"Yes, mam," he said with a dashing smile. "Don't worry, Jack is a friendly horse, but don't let him get close to the other horses. He kicks occasionally."

Rosa was nervous about drawing attention to herself, but Jack behaved and the ride was uneventful. When Curly helped her dismount, he held on longer than he had to, part of the act. Still, she couldn't ignore the flutter of a feeling she couldn't describe.

That night, Angelica met her new fling and soon forgot Rosa was with her. Rosa tried to be content as she sat alone and listened to the music. The Cowboys were in attendance that night. Wyatt looked at Rosa, then at Curly. "Looks like you're up," he said to Curly.

Curly didn't mind asking Rosa to dance. He was 6'4" and usually had trouble finding a dance partner his size. He guessed Rosa was almost six feet tall. She turned beet red, humiliated as he approached her. She wanted to dance but knew he felt obligated to ask. Rosa had a background in dance and followed his country swing with ease. He was a fabulous lead. Rosa couldn't help being swept off her feet. He was funny, friendly, and popular; the little kids adored him. She was certain he had better things to do than dance with her, but they stayed on the dance floor, and within a short time it seemed like they had been practicing for years. Curly understood the position Rosa was in; the D'Augellis were too busy drinking and partying to notice her sitting alone. Curly attended the clubhouse every night to dance with her.

On the last night of her stay, Angelica went to dinner with her new boyfriend. They had spent most of the week together. Rosa didn't mind being alone, and visited the horses in the pasture before dark. She had become fond of Snowball and brought apple slices as a treat.

"Thank you, Snowball. You are such a good girl," she whispered. "I'll never forget you or this vacation, and I hope you'll always be happy." Snowball nuzzled her, grateful for the attention. Rosa turned when she heard someone walking behind her.

"Hi Rosie"

"Hi Curly"

"You've made a friend there Rosie, horses can sense when someone likes them. You two have formed a bond."

Rosa tried to think of something to say since they hadn't talked much at the clubhouse. "How do you like being a cowboy?" she asked.

"It's a summer job, so I can't call myself a cowboy. I don't know if you noticed, but I was not in the rodeo, and they gave me beginner classes."

"Well, what do you do?"

"Besides getting in trouble? I'm a student; I just graduated high school and will attend college next year."

Rosa smiled. He was only two years older.

"How about you, Rosie? Is your next gig bull riding?" he asked jokingly.

"No silly. I will be a junior when school starts, but I'm unsure about college. I might like to attend college out of state and major in biology."

"Interesting subject. I am going into business."

There was a long, comfortable silence between them. Curly knew she was leaving in the morning. He wanted to let her know he had enjoyed the time they spent dancing together.

"I had a good time on the dance floor, Rosie."

Curly looked at Rosa. He liked her. She was quiet and not chatty like most girls her age. When he danced with her, he was aware of a growing attraction. She had an exotic look about her; in her eyes.

He couldn't tell what color they were; they seemed light, sometimes green, sometimes blue. In the fading sunlight, they looked green with a darker blue around her iris and a gold starburst radiating from the center. She was bold enough to hold his gaze. She had a delicate figure, like a dancer. He noticed her lips; they were full and looked soft with just a hint of lip gloss. She was young and sweet; he wanted to hold her and wondered if she had ever been kissed. As he gazed into those mesmerizing eyes, he saw intensity and knew she wanted something from him. They were alone except for Snowball. He felt an unexpected desire as he put his arms around her. She didn't resist. Rosa felt right in his arms as he kissed her gently. Afterward, when she gave him a grateful smile; he realized he had sent the wrong message. They would probably never see each other again, and he wanted her to remember him. Suddenly he longed for a more passionate kiss. She met him halfway as he leaned into her. There was nothing innocent in this kiss. They responded to the embrace, surprised by the intensity. Rosa relaxed, shocked by the powerful longing she felt in his arms. Finally, she pulled away and looked at him with a sad smile.

"Thank you, Curly. I knew there was a reason I came on this trip."

Curley watched her as she turned and walked to her cabin. He was certain she didn't recognize her power and allure. He tended the horses. The taste of strawberry lip gloss lingered on his lips.

About the Author

Joanne Henning (also known as Dr. Szemboski) opened her New Jersey dental practice in 1987. Her passion for storytelling blossomed into novels that blend romance, adventure, and humor against the backdrop of the 1980s. Her titles include *'Faulty Impressions,' Deceptive Images,'* and *'The Platinum Bicuspid'*. She writes under the banner of *'Dental Tales of Love, Adventure, and Fun'*, a unique series about women dentists in the 1980s.

Her books and eBooks are available at your preferred retailer, with audiobooks to launch in 2026. Visit www.dentalromancenovel.com for more information.

A note from the author: If this story brought you a smile or moments of escape, I would love to hear your thoughts. Sharing a review with your preferred retailer helps these light-hearted, dental-themed romances find readers who enjoy them most. Dentistry is the key to the heart!

Made in the USA
Coppell, TX
26 June 2026

82219196R00154